Bantam Books, by Barbara Cartland
Ask your bookseller for the books you have missed

Barbara Cartland's Library of Love

Barbara Cartland's Library of Love

MAN AND MAID
BY ELINOR GLYN
CONDENSED BY
BARBARA CARTLAND

MAN AND MAID
A Bantam Book / November 1977

ISBN 0-553-11370-4

Published simultaneously in the United States and Canada

Bantam Books are published by Bantam Books, Inc. Its trade-
mark, consisting of the words "Bantam Books" and the por-
trayal of a bantam, is registered in the United States Patent
Office and in other countries. Marca Registrada. Bantam
Books, Inc., 666 Fifth Avenue, New York, New York 10019.

PRINTED IN THE UNITED STATES OF AMERICA

Introduction
by
Barbara Cartland

I love this Elinor Glyn novel and for years when I have wished to escape into a quiet yet passionate world of love, I have read *Man and Maid*. No woman could fail to want Sir Nicholas to find happiness with the lovely, distressed, self-sacrificing Alathea. She is everything that is irresistible and feminine, and yet she has character and will-power. There is a lot of inspiration for us all in this love story.

Chapter
One

February, 1918

I am sick of my life. The war has robbed it of all that a young man can find of joy.

I look at my face before I replace the black patch over the left eye, and I realise that with my crooked shoulder, and the leg gone from the right knee downwards, no woman can feel emotion for me again in this world.

Mercifully, I have no near relations—mercifully I am still very rich—mercifully I can buy love when I require it, which, in the circumstances, is not often.

Why do people write journals? Because human nature is filled with egotism. There is nothing so interesting to oneself as oneself.

A clean white page is a sympathetic thing, waiting there to receive one's impressions!

Suzette supped with me, here in my *appartement*, last night. When she had gone I felt a beast. I had found her attractive on Wednesday, and after an excellent lunch and two Benedictines I was able to convince myself that her tenderness and passion were real, and not the result of some thousands of francs.

Then, when she left, I saw my face in the

1

glass without the patch over the socket, and a profound depression fell upon me.

Is it because I am such a mixture that I am this rotten creature? An American grandmother, a French mother, and an English father. Paris, Eton, Cannes. Continuous travelling. Some years of living and enjoying a rich orphan's life. The war, fighting, a zest hitherto undreamed of, unconsciousness, agony, and then? Well, now Paris again for special treatment.

Why do I write this down? For posterity to take up the threads correctly? Why?

I know not, and care not.

Three charming creatures are coming to have tea with me today. They had heard of my loneliness and my savageness from Maurice. They burn to give me their sympathy, and have tea with plenty of sugar in it, and chocolate cake.

When I have seen these three I will dissect them. A divorcée; a war widow of two years; and the third with a husband fighting.

All, Maurice assures me, ready for anything, and highly attractive. It will do me a great deal of good, he protests. We shall see.

Night. They came—with Maurice and Alwood Chester of the American Red Cross. They gave little shrill screams of admiration for the room.

"Yes, the war is much too long. Surely after the spring offensive, peace must come soon—and one must live!" Thus they chattered.

They smoked continuously and devoured the chocolate cake.

They were so well-dressed and so lissom.

They spoke of the theatre, and the last *bon mots*—about their *chères amis*—the last liaisons—the last passions.

Thus they talked.

The widow's lover is married, Maurice tells me, and has been able to keep his wife safely down at their place in Landes; but if peace should come he must be *en famille,* and the wife can very well be disagreeable about the affair.

The divorcée's three lovers will be in Paris at the same time. The married one's husband returned for good. "Yes, certainly peace will have its drawbacks. The war knows its compensations. But considerable ones!"

When they had departed, Burton came into the room to take away the tea things. His face was like a mask as he swept up the cigarette ashes, then he carefully carried away the silver ash trays filled with the ends, and returned with them cleaned. Then he coughed slightly.

"Shall I open the window, Sir Nicholas?"

"It is a beastly cold evening."

He put an extra log on the fire and threw the second casement wide.

"You'll enjoy your dinner better now, Sir," he said, and left me shivering.

* * *

I wish I were a musician, I could play to myself. I have still my two hands, though perhaps my left shoulder hurts too much to play often. My one eye aches when I read for too long, and the stump below the knee is too tender still to fit the false leg onto; and I cannot, because of my shoulder, use my crutch overmuch. So walking is out of the question.

These trifles are perhaps the cause of my ennui with life.

I suppose such women as those who came today fulfil some purpose in the scheme of things.

One can dine openly with them at the most exclusive restaurants, and not mind meeting one's relations. They are rather more expensive than the others. Pearl necklaces, sables, petrol in their motor-cars, these are their prices.

They are seen everywhere, and Coralie, the married one, wears a Red Cross uniform sometimes at tea, if she happens to remember to go into a hospital for ten minutes to hold some poor fellow's hand.

Yes, I suppose they have their uses.

Tomorrow Maurice is bringing another specimen to divert me—American, this time, over here for "war work"; Maurice says she is one of the cleverest adventuresses he has ever met.

Burton is sixty years old. He is my earliest recollection. Burton knows the world.

Friday. The American adventuress delighted me, she was so shrewd. Her eyes are cunning and evil, her flesh is round and firm, she is not extremely painted, and her dresses are quite six inches below her knees.

All these parasites are the produce of war, though probably they always existed, but the war has been their glorious chance.

Are men fools? Yes, imbeciles—they cannot see the wiles of women. Perhaps I could not when I was a human male whom they could love!

Love? Did I say love?

Is there such a thing? Or is it only a sex excitement for the moment? That, at all events, is the sum of what these creatures know.

I cannot now understand how a man marries one of them—gives his name and his honour into such precarious keeping. Once, I suppose, I should have been as easy a prey as the rest. But not now.

Maurice has his uses. Were I a man once more I should despise Maurice. He is so good a creature, such a devoted hanger-on to the very rich—and faithful too. Does he not pander to my every fancy, and procure me whatever I momentarily desire?

How much better if I had been killed outright! I loathe myself and all the world.

Once—before the war—the doing up of this flat caused me raptures. To get it quite English— in Paris! Every *antiquaire* in London had exploited me to their heart's content. I paid for it through the nose—but each bit is a gem.

Nina once proposed to stay with me here— no one would know. . . . Nina?—would she come now? How dare they make this noise at the door —what is it? . . . Nina!

Sunday. It was actually Nina herself. "Poor darling Nicholas," she said. "The kindest fate sent me across. I 'wangled' a passport—really serious war work, and here I am for a fortnight—even in war time one must get a few clothes. . . ."

I could see I was a great shock to her—my attraction for her had gone. I was just "poor darling Nicholas," and she began to be motherly. Nina motherly!

Nina is thirty-nine years old.

She gave me news of the world.

"Why have you completely cut yourself off from everything and everybody ever since you first went out? Very silly of you."

"When I was a *man* and could fight—I liked fighting, and never wanted to see any of you again. You all seemed rotters to me—so I spent my leaves in the country or here. Now you seem glorious beings, and I am the rotter. I am no use at all. . . ."

Nina came close to me and touched my hand. "Poor darling Nicholas," she said again.

Something hurt awfully, as I realised that to touch me now caused her no thrill. No woman will ever thrill again when I am near.

Presently, when she had finished her tea, she said:

"You are absolutely out of gear, Nicholas. Your voice is rasping, your remarks are bitter, and you must be awfully unhappy, poor boy."

I told her that I was—there was no use in lying.

"Everything is finished," I said—and she bent down and kissed me as she said good-bye—a mother's kiss. . . .

And now I am alone, and what shall I do all the evening? or all the other evenings? I will send for Suzette to dine.

Night. Suzette—was amusing. I told her at once I did not require her to be affectionate.

*   *   *

I have been through torture this week. The new man wrenches my shoulder each day—it will become straight eventually, he says.

They have tried to fit the false leg also, so those two things are going on, but the socket is not yet well enough for anything to be done to my left eye—so that has defeated them!

Nina came again, to luncheon this time. It was pouring with rain, an odious day. She told me of her love affairs, as a sister might. Nina a sister!

She can't make up her mind whether to take Jim Bruce or Rochester Moreland—they are both Brigadiers now—Jim is a year younger than she is.

"You are not really in love with either, Nina?"

"Love?" and she smoothed out the fringe on her silk jersey with her war-hardened hand, the hand I once loved to kiss.

"I often wonder what really is love, Nicholas. I thought I loved you before the war, but of course I could not have, because I don't feel anything now, and if I had really loved you I suppose it would not have made any difference."

Then she realised what she had said, and got up and came closer to me.

"You see, we have become so complicated—" she puffed smoke rings at me. "One man does not seem to fulfil the needs of every mood—Rochester would not understand some things that Jim would, and vice versa."

"Will you toss up?"

"No—Rochester is coming up from the front tomorrow just for the night—I am going to dine with him at Larue's—alone, and I shall sample him all the time. I sampled Jim when he was last in London a fortnight ago—"

"You will tell me about it when you have decided, won't you, Nina?"

"Of course I will."

She had her coffee and liqueur—she was graceful and composed and refined. Either Jim or Rochester will have a very nice wife. . . .

* * *

Burton coughed when she had left.

"Out with it, Burton!"

"Mrs Ardilawn is a kind lady, Sir Nicholas."

"Charming."

"I believe you'd be better with some lady to look after you, Sir."

"To hell with you! Telephone for Mr Maurice —I don't want any women. We can play piquet."

That is how my day ended.

Friday. Maurice brings people to play bridge every afternoon now. Nina has gone back to England, having decided to take Jim!

It came about in this way: she flew in to tell me the last evening before she left for Havre.

"Jim and I are engaged!"

"A thousand congratulations."

"Was Rochester upset?"

"Rather, but a man of his age, he is forty-two, is going to get cured soon, so I did not worry."

Burton had brought me in a mild gin and seltzer—and it was on the tray, near—so I drank it, and said to myself: "Here's to Nina!" Then I telephoned to Suzette to come and dine.

* * *

There is a mole on the left cheek of Suzette, high up near her eye—there are three black hairs in it. I had never seen them until this morning— *c'est fini—Je ne peut plus!*

* * *

Of course we have all got moles with three black hairs in them—and the awful moment is when suddenly they are seen. That is the tragedy of life—disillusion.

I cannot help being horribly introspective. Maurice would agree to whatever I said, so there is no use in talking to him—I rush to this journal; it cannot look at me with fond watery eyes of reproach and disapproval—as Burton would if I let myself go to him.

May 16

The times have been too anxious to write, over two months since I opened this book. But it cannot be, it cannot be that we shall be beaten. Oh! God—why am I not a man again to fight! The raids are continuous.

Today the Duchesse de Courville-Hautevine came to call upon me—mounted all the stairs without even a wheeze. What a personality! How I respect her. She has worked magnificently since the war began.

Her hospital is a wonder. Her only son was killed, fighting gloriously at Verdun.

"You look as melancholy as a sick cat," she told me.

She likes to speak her English.

"We are not done yet. War is war—and there is no use in looking blue. Cheer up, young man!"

Then we talked of other things; she is witty and downright, and her every thought and action is kindly. I love *la Duchesse*. My mother was her dearest friend.

When she had stayed twenty minutes, she came over close to my chair.

"I knew you would be bitter at not being in the fight, my son," she said. "*Tiens!* You can at least pray—you have the time!—I have not. *Mais le bon Dieu* understands."

And with that she left me. I felt better after she had gone. Yes, it is that. God—why can't I fight!

Chapter
Two

May, 1918

Is some nerve being touched by the new treatment? I seem alternately to be numb and perfectly indifferent to how the war is going, and then madly interested. But I am too sensitive to leave my flat for any meals.

All sorts of people come to see me—but I seem to be stripping them of externals all the time. What is the good in them? What is the truth in them? Strip me—if I were not rich, what would anyone bother with me for? Is anyone worthwhile underneath?

Oh! the long, long days—and the ugly nights! One does not sleep very well now. The raids at night!—but I believe I grow to like the raids.

Friday. Maurice has a new suggestion—he says I should write a book—he *knows* I am becoming insupportable, and he thinks if he flatters me enough I'll swallow the bait, and so be kept quiet and not try him so much.

I feel a spark of interest. If it could take me out of myself. I shall consult the Duchesse—I will tell Burton to telephone and find out if I can see her this afternoon. She sometimes takes half an hour off between four and five to attend to her family. . . .

Yes—Burton says she will see me and will send one of her Red Cross cars to fetch me, then I can keep my legs up.

I rather incline to a treatise on the philosophical subjects. I fear if I wrote a novel it would be saturated by my ugly spirit, and I should hate people to read it. I must get that part of me off in my journal, but a book about—philosophy? . . .

I must have a shorthand-typist—if I do begin this thing. There are some English ones here, no doubt. I do not wish to write in French. Maurice must find me a suitable one. I won't have anything young and attractive.

In my idiotic state she might get the better of me—the idea of some steady employment quite bucks me up.

* * *

I felt rather jarred when I arrived at the Hotel de Courville—the paving across the river is bad; but I found my way to the Duchesse's own sitting-room on the first floor, the only room apparently left not a ward, and somehow the smell of carbolic had not penetrated there.

A servant in black, verging upon ninety, brought in the tea and said *Madame la Duchesse* would be there immediately, and she came.

Her twinkling eyes kindly as ever. "Good-day, Nicholas," she said, and kissed me on both cheeks.

"You have come for something—out with it!"

"Shall I write a book? That's it. Maurice thinks it might divert me. What do you think?"

"One must consider," and she began pouring

out the tea, "paper is scarce. I doubt, my son, if what you would inscribe upon it would justify the waste—but still—on what subject?"

"That is what I want your advice about—a novel? Or a study on philosophy, or—or—something like that?"

She chuckled and handed me my tea—thin tea and a tiny slice of black bread, and a scrape of butter. There is no cheating of the regulations here, but the Sèvres cup gave me satisfaction.

"You have brought me your bread coupon, I hope?" she interrupted herself with—"If you eat without it, one of my household has less!"

I produced it.

Then she became all interest in my project again, and chuckled anew.

"Not a novel, my son. No! Something serious. No, philosophy it must be—or your pet hobby, the furniture of your William and Mary!"

This seemed the best of all and I decided in a moment. This shall be my subject. I really know something of William and Mary furniture! So we settled it.

Burton is delighted that I shall write a book! I am becoming quite excited. I long to begin, but there is no use until Maurice finds me a short-hand-typist.

He has heard of two, one a Miss Jenkins, aged forty. Sounds good, but she can only give three hours a day, and I must have one at my beck and call.

There is a second one, a Miss Sharp, but she is only twenty-three. Plain, though, Maurice says, and wears horn-rimmed spectacles—that should not attract me! She makes bandages all the evening, but is obliged to work for her living, so could come for the day.

She is not out of a job, because she is very expert, but she does not like her present one.

I would have to pay her very highly, Maurice says—I don't mind that, I want the best. I had better see Miss Sharp and judge if I can stand her. She may have a personality I could not work with. Maurice must bring her tomorrow.

The news tonight is worse.

I picked Maurice up at the Ritz this evening at nine o'clock—there was not a human soul to be seen in the Rue de la Paix, or the Place Vêndôme—a city of the dead. And the early June sky full of peace and soft light.

What does it all mean?

* * *

Maurice brought Miss Sharp today to interview me. I do not like her much, but the exhibition she gave me of her speed and accuracy in shorthand satisfied me and made me see that I should be a fool to look further. So I have engaged her.

She is a small creature, palish, with rather good bright brown hair. She wears horn-rimmed spectacles with yellow glasses in them, so I can't see her eyes at all. I judge people by their eyes.

Her hands look as if she has done rather a lot of hard work—they are so very thin. Her clothes are neat but shabby.

I suppose she is very poor. Her manner is icily quiet. She speaks only when she is spoken to. She is quite uninteresting.

It is better for me to have a nonentity—then I can talk aloud my thoughts without restriction. I am to give her double what she is getting now—two thousand francs a month—war price.

Some colour came into her cheeks when I offered that, and she hesitated.

I said, "Don't you think it is enough?"

She answered so queerly.

"I think it is too much, and I was wondering if I would be able to accept it. I want to."

"Then do."

"Very well. I will, of course, do my best to earn it," and with that she bowed and left me.

Anyhow, she won't make a noise.

Nina writes since she has married Jim—which she did just before the offensive in March.

> "You can't think, Nicholas, what a different aspect the whole war took on when I knew Jim was in the front line. I adore him, and up to now I have managed to keep him adoring me; but I can see I'll have to be careful if he is going to be with me long at a time."

So it would seem that Nina has not obtained the rest and security she hoped for.

I hope my writing a book will rest me. I have arranged all my first chapter in my head, and tomorrow I begin.

June 26

Miss Sharp came punctually at ten. She had a black and white cotton frock on. There is nothing of her, she is so slight (a mass of bones probably in evening dress). She goes at six.

She is to have her lunch here—Burton has arranged it. An hour off for lunch, which she can have on a tray in the small Salon which I have had arranged for her work-room. Of course it won't take her an hour to eat, but Burton says she must have that time, it is always done.

I was full of ideas and the beginning of my first chapter spouted out, and when Miss Sharp had read it over to me I found she had not made any mistakes. That is a mercy.

She went away and typed it, and then had her lunch—and I had mine; but Maurice dropped in and mine took longer than hers—it was half past two when I rang my hand-bell for her. She answered it promptly—the script in her hand.

"I have had half an hour with nothing to do," she said. "Can you not give me some other work which I can turn to, if this should happen again?"

"I might leave you some letters to answer."

"Thank you, that would be best."

We began again.

She sits at a table with her notebook, and while I pause she is absolutely still—that is good. I feel she won't count more than a table or a chair. I am quite pleased with my work.

I am going to have a small dinner tonight, at the Ritz, with Maurice in a private room. It is my birthday—I am thirty-one years old.

Friday. What an evening that twenty-sixth of June! The sirens began, and the guns followed. They seemed unusually loud, and we could hear the bits of shrapnel falling on the terrace beneath us.

Then the dramatic happened. Bang!—the whole house shook and the glass of the window crashed in fragments—and Maurice turned out the one light, and lifted a corner of the thick curtain to peep out.

"I believe they've got the Column Vendôme," he said, awed.

The sight in the hall when we arrived there,

after the "all clear" went, was remarkable—the great glass doors of the Salon blown in and all the windows broken—and the Place Vendôme a mass of debris—not a pane whole there, I should think.

But nobody seems very much upset—these things are all in the day's work.

I said to Miss Sharp this morning:

"What do you do in the evenings when you leave here?"

I had forgotten for a moment that Maurice had told me she made bandages. She looked at me and her manner froze—I can't think why I *felt* she thought I had no right to question her—I say "looked at me" but I am never quite sure what her eyes are doing, because she never takes off her yellow glasses.

Those appeared to be gazing at me, at all events.

"I make bandages."

"Aren't you dead tired after working all day with me?"

"I have not thought about it—the bandages are badly needed."

Her pencil was in her hand, and the block ready. She evidently did not mean to go on conversing with me. This attitude of continuous diligence on her part had begun to irritate me. She never fidgets, just works all the time.

I'll ask Burton what he thinks of her at luncheon today. As I said before, Burton knows the world.

* * *

"What do you think of my typist, Burton?"

"The young lady works very regular."

"Yes, that is just it—a kind of machine."

"She earns her money, Sir Nicholas."

"Of course she does, I know all that. But what do you think of her?"

"Beg pardon, Sir Nicholas, I don't understand."

I felt irritated.

"Of course you do. I mean, what kind of a creature?"

"The young lady doesn't chatter, Sir—she doesn't behave like bits of girls."

"You approve of her then, Burton?"

"She's been here a fortnight only, Sir Nicholas—you can't tell in that time." That is all I could get out of him, but I felt the verdict when he did give it would be favourable.

Insignificant little Miss Sharp!

What shall I do with my day? I have no more inspiration for my book—besides, Miss Sharp has to type the long chapter I gave her yesterday. I wonder if she knows anything about William and Mary furniture really.

Her hands are very red these last days—does making bandages redden the hands?

I wonder what colour her eyes are—one can't tell with that dark yellow glass. . . .

Suzette came in just as I wrote that; she seldom turns up in the afternoon. She caught sight of Miss Sharp typing through the open door.

"*Tiens!*" she spat at me. "Since when?"

"I am writing a book, Suzette."

"I must see her face." And without waiting for permission, Suzette flounced into the small Salon.

I could hear her shrill little voice asking Miss Sharp to be so good as to give her an envelope

—she must write an address. I watched—Miss
Sharp handed her one, and went on with her
work.

Suzette returned, closing the door, without
temper, behind her.

"Wouff!" she announced to me—"no anxiety
there—an *Anglaise*—not appetising—as thin as a
hairpin! Nothing for you, Nicholas—and, *mon
Dieu!* she does the family washing, by her hands."

"You think it is washing? I was wondering—"

"Does she take off her glasses ever, Nicholas?"

"No—perhaps she has weak light eyes. One
never can tell!"

Suzette was not yet quite at ease about it all.

Suzette showed affection for me after this—
and even passion. I would be quite good-looking,
she said—when I should be finished—glass eyes
were so well made now—"and as for legs!"

Of course I felt comforted when she had
gone.

*   *   *

The hot days pass. Miss Sharp has not asked
for a holiday; we do a great deal of work and she
writes all my letters. And there are days when I
know I am going to be busy with my friends,
when I tell her she need not come. There was a
whole week in July.

Her manner never alters, but when Burton
attempted to pay her she refused to take the
cheque.

"I did not earn that," she said.

I was angry with Burton because he did not
insist, so I spoke to Miss Sharp myself.

"It was my business as to whether I worked or

did not work for a week, therefore you are owed payment in any case. That is logic—"

A queer red came into her transparent skin, and her mouth shut firmly. I knew that I had convinced her, and that yet for some reason she hated having to take the money.

She did not even answer, just bowed with that strange aloofness that is not insolent. Her manner is never like a person of the lower classes, trying to show she thinks she is an equal.

It has exactly the right note—perfectly respectful as one who is employed, but with the serene unselfconsciousness that only breeding gives.

I have not seen my dear Duchesse lately—she has been down to one of her country places where she sends her convalescents, but she is returning soon—she gives me pleasure.

* * *

August

The interest in the book has flagged lately. I could not think of a thing, so I proposed to Miss Sharp to have a holiday—she accepted the fortnight without enthusiasm. Now she is back and we have begun again. Still I have no *flair*. Why do I stick to it?

Just because I have said to the Duchesse that I *will* finish it? ... I have an uneasy feeling that I do not want to probe my real reason—I would like to lie even to this journal.

Perhaps it is Miss Sharp who irritates me with her eternal diligence. What is her life? Who are her family? I would like to know, but I will not ask.

Her hair is pretty—that silky sort of nut brown with an incipient wave in it; her head is set on most gracefully, I must admit, and the complexion is very pale and transparent. The hands are well shaped.

How long would it take to get them white again? I wonder. She has got good feet too, thin like the hands. How worn her clothes look—does she never have a new dress?

* * *

God! What is the meaning of it all?

I have been in hell ... I came in from my drive very quietly—it was early—a quarter to six —Miss Sharp goes at six. It was a horribly chilly evening and Burton had lit a bright wood fire— and I suppose its crackling prevented my hearing the sounds which were coming from the next room for a minute.

I sat down in my chair.

What was that?—the *roucoulements* of a dove? No, a woman's voice cooing foolish love words in French and English—and a child's treble gurgling fondness back to her.

I sat and listened, and suddenly I felt my cheek wet with tears—then some shame, some anger shook me, and I started up, got my crutch, and hobbled to the door.

I opened it wide. There was Miss Sharp with the concierge's daughter's baby on her lap, fondling it—the creature may be six months old. Miss Sharp's horn spectacles lay on the table. She looked up at me, the slightest flush of timidity showing, but her eyes—oh!

God, the eyes of the Madonna, heavenly blue, tender as an angel's, soft as a doe's! I could have cried aloud with some pain in the soul, and so that brute part of me spoke—

"How dare you make this noise?" I said rudely. "Do you not know that I have given orders for complete quiet?"

She rose, holding the child with the greatest dignity. The picture she made could be in the Sistine Chapel.

"I beg your pardon," she said in a voice which was not quite steady. "I did not know you had returned, and Madame Bizot asked me to hold little Augustine while she went to the next floor. It shall not occur again!"

I longed to stay and gaze at them both. I would have liked to touch the baby's queer little fat fingers—I would have liked—oh! I know not what.

And all the time Miss Sharp held the child protectively, as though something evil would come from me and harm it. Then she turned and carried it out of the room and I went back into my sitting-room and flung myself down in my chair.

What had I done, beast! Brute! What had I done?

And will she never come back again? And will life be emptier than ever?

I could kill myself.

Chapter
Three

This morning I feel as if I could hardly bear it until Miss Sharp arrives. I dressed early, ready to begin a new chapter, although I have not an idea in my head, and, as the time grows nearer, it is difficult for me to remain still here in my chair.

Have I been too impossible? Will she not turn up?—and if she does not, what steps can I take to find her?

I do not know Miss Sharp's home address —nor if she has a telephone—probably not. My heart beats—I have every feeling of excitement, as stupid as a woman.

She came after all, only ten minutes beyond her usual time, but they seemed an eternity when I heard the ring and Burton's slow step.

She came in and up to my chair as usual, but she did not say her customary cold good-morning. Her eternal pad and pencil were in her little thin, red hands.

"Good-morning," I said tentatively. She made a slight inclination.

"Er—would you read me aloud the last chapter we finished?" I barked at last lamely.

She turned to fetch the script from the other room.

I must apologise to her, I knew.

She came back and sat down stiffly, prepared to begin.

"I am sorry I was such an uncouth brute yesterday," I said. "It was good of you to come back. Will you forgive me?"

She bowed again. I almost hated her at that moment, she was making me feel so much.

"We had better get to work, I suppose," I went on.

She began to read. How soft her voice is, and how perfectly cultivated! The music of her reading calmed me—how I wish we could be friends!

"How old is Madame Bizot's grandchild?" I asked abruptly, interrupting.

"Ten months," answered Miss Sharp without looking up.

"You like children?"

"Yes."

"Perhaps you have some brothers and sisters?"

"Yes."

"How many?"

"Two."

The tone said, "I consider your questions impertinent."

I went on—

"Brothers?"

"One brother."

"And a sister?"

"Yes."

"How old?"

"Eleven and thirteen."

"That is quite a gap between your ages, then?"

She did not think it necessary to reply to this.

There was no sign of nervousness in Miss Sharp's manner. I simply did not exist for her. As a man I had no meaning—as a wounded human being she had no pity for me—but I did not want her pity. What did I want?

I cannot write it—I cannot face it. Am I to have a new torment in my life? Desiring the unattainable? Need it always be so? I wish to God I knew.

Night. She worked with her usual diligence the entire day almost, not taking the least notice of me—until at five o'clock, when my tea came in, I rang for her. I asked her to pour out the tea.

"If you will be so very kind," I said—"I have let Burton go out."

When she was near me I felt happier, for some reason.

She asked me how I took my tea, and I told her.

"Are you not going to have some with me?" I pleaded.

"Mine is already on my table in the next room—thank you," and she rose.

In desperation I blurted out—

"Please—do not go! I don't know why, but I feel most awfully rotten today."

She sat down again and poured out her cup.

"If you are suffering, shall I read to you?" she said. "It might send you to sleep," and somehow I fancied that while her firm mouth never softened, perhaps the eyes behind the horn spectacles might not be so stony.

"Please read," I said in desperation, and I closed my one eye.

She picked up a book and read at random. The last thing I remember was hearing her voice, and when I woke it was past six o'clock and she had gone home.

Suzette came to dinner—I thought how vulgar she looked, and that if her hands were white they were podgy and the nails short.

"Amuse me!" I commanded.

"So it is not love then, Nicholas, thou desirest?"

"Not in the least; I shall never want love again, probably. Divert me!—tell me of your scheming little mouse's brain, and your kind little heart."

"I hope to buy a farm for my mother and I shall put Georgine into a convent for the nobility."

"Who is Georgine? You have not spoken of her before, Suzette."

She reddened a little under her new terra-cotta rouge.

"No? Oh! Georgine is my little first mistake, but I have her beautifully brought up, Nicholas—with the Holy Mother at St. Brieux—I am then her aunt, so to speak—the wife of a small shop-keeper in Paris, you must know."

Something touched me infinitely. This queer little demi-mondaine mother—her thoughts set on her child's purity.

I respect Suzette far more than my friends of the world.

When she left—it was perhaps in bad taste, but I gave her a quite heavy four-figure cheque.

"For the education of Georgine, Suzette."

She flung her arms round my neck and

kissed me on both cheeks, and tears were brimming over in her merry black eyes.

Wednesday. For two days after I last wrote I tried not to see Miss Sharp. I gave short moments to my book, and she answered a number of business letters. She knows most of my affairs now; Burton transmits all the bills and papers to her.

Finally, I deliberately rang my bell, and when she came into the room I found I was not sure what I had rung for. It is the most exasperating fact that Miss Sharp keeps me in a continual state of nervous consciousness.

Her manner was indifferently expectant, if one can use such a paradoxical description.

"I—I—wondered if you played the piano," I blurted out.

She looked surprised—if one can ever say she looks anything, with the expression of her eyes completely hidden.

"Yes."

"I suppose you would not play to me?—er—it might give me an inspiration for the last chapter."

She went and opened the lid of the instrument.

"What sort of music do you like?" she asked.

"Play whatever you think I would appreciate."

She began the "1812."

The same feeling came over me that I experienced when I heard the cooing of the child. My nerves must be in an awfully rotten state.

I started to shift my one leg and the frightful pain of my sudden movement did me good—and steadied me.

Miss Sharp left the piano and came over to me.

"I am afraid you did not like that," she said.

"Yes, I did," I answered. "Forgive me for being an awful ass. I—I—love music tremendously, you see—"

She stood still for a moment—I was balancing myself by the table, for my crutch had fallen. Then she put out her hand.

"Can I help you to sit down again?" she suggested.

And I let her—I wanted to feel her touch. But when I felt her guiding me to the chair, the maddest desire to seize her came over me—to seize her in my arms—to tear off those glasses, to kiss those beautiful blue eyes they hid.

To hold her fragile scrap of a body tight against my breast, to tell her that I loved her—and wanted to hold her there, mine and no one else's in all the world. . . .

When I was settled in the chair again, things seemed to become black for a minute, and then I heard Miss Sharp's voice with a tone—could it be of anxiety?—in it saying, "Drink this brandy, please."

I took it.

Again I said, "I am awfully sorry I am such an ass."

"If you are all right now, I ought to go back to my work," she remarked.

I nodded, and she went softly from the room. When I was alone, I used every bit of my will to calm myself—I analysed the situation. Miss Sharp loathes me—I cannot hold her by any means if she decides to go.

The only way I can keep her near me is by

continuing to be the cool employer, and to do this I must see her as little as possible—because the profound disturbance she is able to cause in me reacts upon my raw nerves, and I am bound to make a consummate fool of myself.

The Duchesse returned yesterday. I shall go and see her this afternoon, I think—perhaps she could suggest some definite, useful work I could do.

She was so pleased to see me.

"Nicholas! You are better!" she said. "As I told you, the war is going to end well!

"And how is the book?" she asked presently. "It should be finished—I am told, though, that your work is intermittent."

My mind jumped to Maurice as the connecting link.

"You are content with your secretary?"

This was said with an air of complete indifference.

"Yes. She is wonderfully diligent—it is impossible to dislodge her for a moment from her work. She thinks me a poor creature, I expect."

The Duchesse's eyes, half-closed now, were watching me keenly.

"Why should she think that, Nicholas? You can't, after all, fight."

"No—but—"

"Get well, my boy—and these silly introspective fancies will leave you."

And then with a total change of subject she remarked—

"You are not in love, Nicholas?"

I felt a hot flush rise to my face. What an idiotic thing to do!

"In love!" I laughed a little angrily. "With whom could I possibly be in love, *chère amie?*

There would be no use in my being in love, Duchesse."

"It would depend upon the woman—you want sympathy and a guiding hand."

She was called away then, back to one of the wards—and I hobbled down the beautiful staircases by myself.

A slight wisp of a figure passed along the end of a corridor. I could not see plainly, but I could have sworn it was Miss Sharp—I called her name, but no one answered me.

Miss Sharp and the Duchesse! Why, if this is so, have I never been told about it? In the meantime I think I shall go to Versailles. I cannot stand Paris any longer.

Chapter
Four

How I love Versailles.

Why did I not come here sooner? I am at peace with the world. Burton wheels me up onto the terrace every evening to watch the sunset from the top of the great steps.

Suzette suggested that she should come and stay the weekend out here. She wants change of air, she says. I have consented. Miss Sharp does not bring her eternal block and pencil until Tuesday—when Suzette will have left.

Suzette arrived in an entirely new set of garments—the fashion had altered, she said; one had to have a different look.

"The only unfortunate part is that it obliged me to break into the sum for Georgine's education."

"That is at least reparable," I answered, and reached for my cheque-book. Suzette is such a good little sort—and clothes give her pleasure—and fancy being able to give *real pleasure* for a few thousand francs.

She prattled gaily—then when no one was looking she slipped her hand into mine.

30

"*Mon cher! Mon petit chou!*" she said.

We had the gayest dinner in my sitting-room.

I wished then that I had made the cheque larger—because of her merry black eyes.

... I wonder if material things could affect Miss Sharp. What can she think about all day?—certainly not my affairs—attending to them must be purely mechanical. I know she is not stupid.

She plays beautifully—she thinks—she has an air, and knowledge of the world.

Suzette left last evening in the best of moods—I made the cheque larger—and now I am awaiting Miss Sharp in my sitting-room. I love this hotel—it has an air of indifference about it which is soothing, and the food is excellent.

* * *

Miss Sharp arrived about eleven today. Her cheeks were quite pink when she came in, and I could see she was warm from walking. I wish I had remembered to send to the station to meet her.

"Do you think we shall be able to work here?" I asked her.

"Why not here as well as any other place?"

"Does not environment matter to you?"

"I suppose it would if I were creating."

"Do you ever write?"

"I write a journal."

"Why does one write a journal?" I wanted to hear what she would answer.

"One writes journals if one is lonely."

"Yes, that is true. Then you are lonely?"

Again she conveyed to me the impression that I had shown bad taste in asking a personal question.

"You explain to me why one writes journals, and then when I presume upon the inference, you snub me. You are not fair, Miss Sharp."

"It would be better to stick to business," was all she answered. "Will you dictate, please?"

I was utterly exasperated.

"No, I won't! If you only admit by inference that you are lonely, I say it right out—I am abominably lonely this morning, and I want to talk to you. Did I see you at the Duchesse de Courville-Hautevine's on Wednesday last?"

"Possibly."

I literally had not the pluck to ask her what she was doing there. However, she went on—

"There are still many wounded who require bandages."

That was it! Of course—she was bringing bandages!

"She is a splendid woman, the Duchesse; she was a friend of my mother's.

"I feel you have a hundred interesting things to say, if you would only talk!" I blurted out.

"I am not here to talk, Sir Nicholas—I am here to do your typing."

"Does that make a complete barrier? Won't you be friends with me?"

Burton came into the room at that moment, and while he was there she slipped off to her typing without answering me. Burton has arranged a place for her in his room, which is next to mine, so that I shall not be disturbed by the noise of her machine clicking.

"Miss Sharp must lunch with me," I said.

Burton coughed as he answered—

"Very good, Sir Nicholas."

That meant that he did not approve of this arrangement—why?

The antediluvian waiters came in to lay the table presently, and I ordered peaches and grapes and some very special Chablis—I felt exultant at my having manoeuvred that Miss Sharp should eat with me!

She came in when all was ready with her usual serene calm, and took her place at right angles to me.

We talked of French politics—that is, she answered everything I said with intelligence, and then let the subject drop immediately.

Then I began about French literature. Oh!—what a companion she would make, if only I could break down this wretched barrier of her reserve!

She ate a peach—and I do hope she liked it.

"Do you know, I believe I shall have my new eye put in before Christmas!" I told her just before she rose from the table—and for the first time since I have known her, the faintest smile came round her mouth—a kindly smile.

"I am so very glad," she said.

And all over me there crept a thrill of pleasure.

After lunch I suggested the *parc*, and that I dictate in some lovely cool spot. She made no objection, but immediately put on her hat—a plain dark-blue straw.

"Does not this place interest you awfully?" I hazarded.

"Yes, but it is ever a reminder of what to avoid."

"What to avoid! But it is perfectly beautiful. Why should you want to avoid beauty? Tell me what you mean."

"The architects were great, the King's

thought was great—but they put false values upon everything—false values upon birth and breeding—and no value upon their consequent obligations, or upon character."

"You believe in acknowledging your obligations, I know."

"Yes, I hope so. Think, in that palace the immense importance which was given to etiquette and ceremonies—and to a quite ridiculous false sense of honour—they could ruin their poor tradesmen and—yet—"

"Yes—" I interrupted, "it was odd, wasn't it?—a gentleman was still a gentleman, never paying his tailor's bills, but ceased to be one if he cheated at cards."

Miss Sharp suddenly dropped her dark blue parasol and bent to pick it up again and as she did so she changed the conversation.

Burton puffed a little as we went up the rather steep slope by the Aile du Nord and Miss Sharp put her hand on the bar to help him push the chair.

"Is it not hateful for me being such a burden," I could not help saying.

"It leaves you more time to think."

"Well! That is no blessing. That is the agony —thinking."

"It should not be. To have time to think must be wonderful!" She sighed unconsciously.

Over me came a kind of rush of tenderness. I wanted to be strong again, and protect her and make her life easy, and give her time and love and everything in the world she could wish for.

She went directly from the *parc* to catch her train at five o'clock and I was wheeled back to the hotel.

And now I have the evening alone before me,

but the day is distinctly a step onward in the friendship line.

* * *

I spent a memorable day with Miss Sharp in the *parc* yesterday. This Thursday will always stand out as a landmark in our acquaintance.

We drove to the Little Trianon, and I walked with my crutch to a delicious spot I know, rather near the grotto, and yet with a view of the house. I was determined I would do as much as I could to entice her to talk.

She was in profile to me so that I could see that her very long eyelashes seemed to be rather pressed against the glasses—I have not before been so close to her in a bright light. "Why does she wear those damned spectacles?" I was thinking, when she said—

"You find it hard to be confined to your chair and not to be able to fight, don't you? Well, when you could fight, it was not always the pleasure of going over the top. You had bad times in the trenches too, hadn't you—when you just had to bear it?"

"Of course."

"Well, you are in the trenches now, don't you see, and it is according to how your soul learns the lesson of them, whether in this life you will ever be allowed to go over the top again, or even to have peace."

"What qualities do you most admire in a person, Miss Sharp?"

"Self-control and strength."

"You have no sympathy with weaklings?"

"None whatever—bad strong people are better than weak good ones."

I knew this was true. This fragile creature

suggests infinite repose and strength. What could she have done in a former life to bring her back in such unkind surroundings, that she must spend her days in drudgery, so that she has never even leisure to think? I longed to ask her, but did not dare.

"Shall we not begin work now?" she suggested, and I demonstrated my first lesson in self-control by agreeing.

"If you don't mind, we will go to the little café by the *lac*," I said, "and then afterwards we can find another place and work again. Burton will have had my wheeled chair brought down there."

As I moved I slipped in the slightest degree, and caught on to her arm. It was bare to the elbow in the little cheap cotton frock, and as I touched the fine, fine skin, that maddening feeling came over me again to clasp her in my arms.

She has a darling tiny curl which comes behind her ear—slipped down probably because her hair is so unfashionably dressed.

Now that I see her out-of-doors and in perspective, I realise that she has a lovely small figure and everything is in the right place. I had told Burton to order the nicest lunch he could think of in that simple place.

I tried to make conversation at lunch. There is nothing in the world so difficult as to keep this up when you are nervous with interest and the other person is determined not to say a sentence which is unnecessary. A chill crept over me.

Burton turned up in time to pay the bill and put me into my chair. He bent over me—

"It would be good for you to be taking a nap, Sir Nicholas. Indeed it would."

It seemed as if Miss Sharp was abetting him, for she came to my side.

"If you can get quite comfortable I would read to you and you might sleep," she said.

"We've no book," I retorted, peeved, and yet pleased at the idea.

"I have one here which will do," and she took a little volume from her bag.

It was a worn eighteenth-century copy of François Villon.

"Yes, that will be nice," I agreed, and leaned back, while Burton settled my cushion and then retired to a distance.

Miss Sharp took a little *parc* chair and I was able to watch her as she read. I did not even hear the words, because as she was looking down, I had not to guard myself, but could let my eyes devour her small oval face.

All my nerves were thrilling again and there was no peace. How I longed—ached—to take her into my arms!

She looked up once after an hour to see if I was asleep, I suppose. She must have observed passionate emotion in my eye. She looked back down at the book instantly, but a soft pink flush came into her cheeks, which have a mother-of-pearl transparency usually.

This caused me deep pleasure. I had been able to make her feel something at any rate, but then I was frightened. Perhaps she would suggest going if she found the situation uncomfortable.

Her voice had a fresh tone in it as she went on, but finally her voice faltered and she stopped reading to me.

"If it is not putting you to sleep," she remarked, "perhaps you would not object if I walked on, and typed what I took down this morning. It seems a pity to waste this time."

I knew that if I did not let her have her way there might be difficulties, so I agreed and said that I would go back to the hotel and rest upon the sofa in the Salon.

But when I got there I heard no typing, only there was a note from Miss Sharp to say that some slight thing had gone wrong with the machine, so she had taken the work to finish it at home.

I cursed and then in pain lay down upon my bed.

Saturday. Yesterday I was so restless I could not settle to anything. My mind was absorbed with thoughts of Miss Sharp.

If I only dared to be natural with her and use my habitual methods with women we surely could be friends, but I am always obsessed with the fear that she will leave me if I transgress in the slightest beyond the line she has marked between us.

I see that she is determined to remain only the secretary, and I realise that it is her breeding which makes her act as she does. If she were familiar or friendly with me, she would feel it was not correct to come to my flat alone.

She comes at all only because the money is so necessary to her—and having to come, she protects her dignity by wearing this ice mask.

Now what is to be done next? I would like to go and confide in the Duchesse, and tell her that I believe I have fallen in love with my secretary, who won't look at me, and ask her advice— but I fear that with all her broad-minded charity, the Duchesse's class prejudice is too strong to make her really sympathetic.

Her French mind of the Ancien Régime could not contemplate a Thormonde—son of Anne de Mont-Anbin—falling in love with an insignificant Miss Sharp who brings bandages to the Courville hospital!

I am dawdling over this last chapter of my book on purpose—and I have reread the former ones and decided to rewrite one or two, but at best I cannot spread all this out over more than six weeks, I fear, and then what excuse can I have for keeping her?

I feel that she would not stay just to answer a few letters a day, and do the accounts and pay the bills with Burton. I feel more desperately miserable than I have felt since last year.

Night. Today was one of utter disaster, although it began fairly well. Miss Sharp turned up at eleven as I shut my journal. She brought all the work she had taken away with her on Thursday, quite in order, and her face wore the usual mask.

I wonder, if I had not ever seen her without her glasses, should I have realised now that she is very pretty?

I can see her prettiness even with them on —her nose is so exquisitely fine, and the mouth a Cupid's bow really—if one can imagine a Cupid's bow very firm. I am sure if she were dressed well she would be lovely.

This morning, when she first came, I began thinking of this, and of how I would like her to have some sapphire bangles for those little wrists and a great string of pearls round that little throat —my mother's pearls—and perhaps big pearls in those shell-like ears.

And how I would like to take her hair down and brush it out, and let it curl as it wanted to, and then bury my face in it—those stiff twists must take heaps of hair to make.

But why am I writing all this when the reality is further off than ever—and indeed has become an impossibility, I fear.

We worked in the sitting-room—it was a cloudy day—and presently, after I had been dreaming on in this way, I asked her to read over the earlier chapters of the book. She did.

"Now what do you think of the thing as a whole?" I asked her.

She was silent for a moment, as though trying not to have to answer directly, then that weird constitutional honesty seemed to force out the words—

"It perhaps tells what that furniture is."

"You feel it is awful rot?"

"No—"

"What then?"

"It depends if you meant to publish it."

I leaned back and laughed—bitterly. I had the exasperated feeling that I was just being pandered to, humoured by everyone, because I was wounded. I was an object of pity, and even my paid typist . . . but I can't write about it.

Miss Sharp started from her chair—her fine nostrils were quivering, and her mouth had an expression I could not place.

"Indeed, it is not bad," she said. "You misunderstand me."

I knew that she was angry with herself for having hurt me, and that I could have made capital out of this, but something in me would not let me do that.

"Oh, it is all right," I replied, but perhaps my voice may have been flat and discouraged, for she went on— so kindly:

"You know a great deal about the subject, of course; but I feel the chapters want condensing. May I tell you just where?"

I felt that the thing did not interest me any more, one way or another. I unconsciously put my head back against the cushion of my chair in weariness. I felt the soft silk and shut my eye for a moment.

When Miss Sharp spoke again, her voice was full of sympathy—and was it remorse?

"I would like to help you to take interest in it again. Won't you let me?" she pleaded.

I was grateful that she did not say she was sorry she had hurt me. That I could not have stood.

I opened my eye now and looked at her. She was bending nearer to me but I felt nothing particular, only a desire to go to sleep and have done with it all.

"It is very good of you," I answered politely. "Yes, say what you think."

Her tact is immense: she plunged straight into the subject without further imputation of sympathy.

She spoke so intelligently, showing trained critical faculties—and at last my numbness began gradually to melt, and I could not help some return of sensation.

There may have been soothing syrup in the fact that she must have been interested in the work, or she could not have dissected it chapter by chapter, point by point, as she was doing.

She grew animated as we discussed things, and once unconsciously she took off her glasses! It was like the sun coming out after days of storm clouds—her beautiful, beautiful blue eyes!

I felt a strange emotion of excitement and

pleasure—I had not time to control my admiration—I expect—for she took fright and instantly replaced them, a bright flush in her cheeks, and went on talking in a more reserved way. Alas!

Of course, then I realised that she does not wear the glasses for any reason of softening light or of defective sight, but simply to hide those blue stars and to make herself unattractive.

How mysterious it all is!

I began to feel that I might write the fool of a book right over from the beginning, and suggested to her that we should take it in detail.

She acquiesced.

Then it suddenly struck me that she had not only spoken of style in writing, but had shown an actual knowledge of the subject of the furniture itself.

How could little Miss Sharp, a poverty-stricken typist, be familiar with William and Mary furniture?

Could she have studied furniture in museums?

But the war has been on for four years and I have gathered that she has been in Paris all that time.

Even if she had left England in 1914—she could only have been eighteen or nineteen then, and girls of that age do not generally take an interest in furniture. This thought kept bothering me, and I was silent for some moments.

I knew that I could disconcert her, and probably obtain some interesting admissions from her, but some instinct warned me not to do so.

I might win out for the time being, but if she has a secret which she does not wish me to discover, she will take care not to again put herself in a situation where this can happen.

However, I registered a vow then that I would find out all I could from Maurice.

The inference of everything she says, does, and unconsciously implies is that she is a cultivated lady, accustomed to talking with people of our world—people who know England and its great houses well.

And yet—she is meanly dressed—does housework—and for years has been trained in professional business methods. It is profoundly interesting.

Well, I write all this down calmly, the record of the morning, to let myself look back on it, and to where the new intimacy might have led us, but for the sickening end to the day.

Burton did not question her lunching with me this time—he had given the order as a matter of course.

By the time the waiters came in to lay the table, that sense of hurt, and then of numbness, had worn off. I was quite interested again in the work, and intensely intrigued with the possibility of extracting from her the history of the Sharp family!

I was using cunning too, and displaying casual indifference, so watchfulness was allowed to rest a little with the strange girl.

"I believe if you will give me your help I shall be able to make quite a decent book of it, after all. You know England well?"

"Yes."

"If it is not a frightfully impertinent question —how old are you really, Miss Sharp?"

I felt that she could not be only twenty-three after this conversation. She smiled—the second smile I have seen.

"On the twentieth of October I shall be twenty-four."

"Where on earth did you learn all your philosophy of life in such short time!"

"It is life which teaches us everything—if we are not half-asleep—especially if it is difficult."

"And the stupid people are like me—not liking to learn any lessons, and kicking against the pricks."

"Yes."

"I would try to learn anything you would teach me, though, Miss Sharp."

"I have not time."

I looked at her as she said this; there was in the tone a faint echo of regret, so I wanted to see the expression of her mouth. It told me nothing.

I could not get anything further out of her, because the waiters came in and out after this rather frequently, changing the courses, and so I did not have any success.

After lunch I suggested that, as it had cleared up, we should go at least as far as the parterre, and sit under the shadow of the terrace.

Miss Sharp followed my bath-chair and with extreme diligence kept me to the rearranging of the first chapter.

For an hour I watched her darling small face whenever I could. A sense of peace was upon me. We were certainly on the first rung of the ladder of friendship, and presently, presently, if only I could keep from annoying her in any way . . . !

When we had finished our task, she rose.

"If you don't mind, as it is Saturday I have promised Burton . . ." and she looked at him, seated on a chair beyond earshot, enjoying the sun, "to do up the accounts and prepare the cheques for you to sign. So I will go in now and begin."

After a few paces she came back again.

"May I ask Burton for the bread ticket I lent you on Thursday?" she said. "No one can afford to be generous with them now, can they!"

I was delighted at this. I would have been delighted at anything which kept her with me an extra minute.

I watched her as she disappeared and then I must have dozed for a while, because it was a quarter to five when I got back to my sitting-room.

And when I was safely in my chair there was a knock on the door, and in she came—with a cheque-book in her hand. Before I opened it or even took it up, I knew something had happened which had changed her again.

Her manner had its old icy respect as of a person employed—all the friendliness which had been growing in the last two or three days had completely departed. I could not imagine why.

She put the cheque-book open and handed me a pen to sign with, and I signed the dozen that she had filled in, and tore them off as I did so.

She was silent, and when I had finished she took them, saying casually that she would bring the corrected chapter typed again on Tuesday, and was now going to catch her train—and before I could reply she had gone into the other room.

A frightful sense of depression fell upon me. What could it possibly be?

Idly I picked up the cheque-book and absently fingered the leaves, then my eye caught a counterfoil where I had chanced to open it.

It was not in Miss Sharp's handwriting, although this was the house cheque-book which Burton usually keeps, but in my own, and there was written, just casually as I scribble in my private account: "For Suzette, 5,000 francs," and the date of last Saturday.

And on turning the page there was the further one: "For Suzette, 3,000 francs," and the date of Monday!

The irony of fate! I had inadvertently, I suppose, on these two days picked up this cheque-book instead of my own.

Chapter
Five

It is quite useless for me to comment upon the utterly annoying circumstance of that mix-up of cheque-books. Such things are fate.

Well, what is the use of writing about it. I am so utterly mad and resentful that I have no words.

It is Sunday morning, and this afternoon I shall hire the one motor which can be obtained here, at a fabulous price, and go into Paris.

But this morning I shall go and sit in the parish church and hear Mass. I feel so completely wretched, the music may comfort me.

The organ was not bad—and before I came out I felt calmer.

After all, it is absurd of Miss Sharp to be disgusted about Suzette. She must know, at nearly twenty-four, and living in France, that there are Suzettes—and I am sure she is not narrow-minded in any way.

What can have made her so censorious? If she took a personal interest in me it would be different, but indifferent as she is, how can it matter to her?

* * *

Monday. Sunday was a memorable day.

I went through the Bois de Marne on that bad road because the trees were so lovely, and then through the Parc de St Cloud.

When we got across the river into the Bois de Boulogne it seemed as if all Paris was enjoying a holiday. I told the chauffeur to go down a side *allée* and to go slowly—and presently I made him draw up at the side of the road.

It was so hot, and I wanted to rest for a little —the motion was jarring my leg.

I think I must have been half-asleep, when my attention was caught by three figures coming up another bypath obliquely; the tallest of them was undoubtedly Miss Sharp—but Miss Sharp as I had never seen her before!

And a boy of thirteen and a girl of eleven were at either side of her—the boy clinging on to her arm—he was lame and seemed to be a dreadfully delicate person.

The little girl was very small and sickly-looking too, but Miss Sharp—my secretary!—appeared blooming and young and lovely in her inexpensive frock. No glasses hid her blue eyes.

Her hair was not torn back and screwed into a knot, and her hat, the simplest thing possible, was most becoming.

Refinement and perfect taste proclaimed themselves from every inch of her, even if everything had cost only a small sum.

So that dowdy get-up is for my benefit, and is not habitual to her! Or is it that she has only one costume and keeps it for Sundays and dates of fête?

In spite of my determination to put all thought of her from me, a wild emotion arose— a passionate longing to spring from the car and join her, to talk to her, and tell her how lovely I thought she was looking.

They came nearer and nearer. I could see that her face was rippling with smiles at something the little brother had said. Its expression was gentle and sympathetic, and it was obvious that fond affection held all three.

As they got close to me I could hear him cough in the hollow way which tells its own story.

When they had gone by, I started forward again to watch them. I could hear the little girl cry, "Oh! look, Alathea!" as she pointed to the sky —and then all three began to quicken their pace in the direction of the Auteuil—and were soon out of sight.

Then, still quivering with emotion, I too glanced heavenwards. Ye Gods! what a storm was coming on.

Where were they going? There into the deep wood? They would be soaked to the skin when the rain did begin to fall—and there was a thunderstorm approaching also—were they quite safe?

All these thoughts tormented me, and I gave the chauffeur orders to take a road I thought might cut across the path they had followed; and when we reached the spot, I made him wait.

The vivid lightning rent the sky and the thunder roared like guns.

My chauffeur complained audibly as he got down to shut the car.

Still I waited, but no Sharp family appeared, and at last I knew I had missed them somehow— a very easy thing in that path-bisected wood. It was one of the worst thunderstorms I have ever seen in my life.

I was horribly worried as to what could have

happened to the little party. They must have got soaking wet—if nothing worse had happened to them! And how could I hear anything about them?

What should I do? Was the Duchesse in Paris? Could I find the address possibly from her? But would she be likely to know it, just because Miss Sharp—"Alathea"—(what a lovely Greek name!) brought bandages to the hospital?

However, this was worth trying, and I could hardly wait to get to the telephone.

How I cursed my folly in not having asked Miss Sharp herself for her address! Could Burton possibly know it? How silly of me not to have thought of that before!

"Burton, I saw Miss Sharp and her family in the Bois. Do you know their address, by chance? I want to ring up and find out if they got home all right."

Burton could see my anxiety, and actually hurried in his reply!

"They live in Autueil, Sir Nicholas, but I can't exactly say where—the young lady never seems very particular to give me the address. She said I should not be needing it, and that they were likely to move."

"Get on to the Duchesse de Courville-Hautevine as quickly as you can."

Burton did so at once, but it seemed a long time.

No, *Madame la Duchesse* was down at Hautevine taking some fresh convalescents and would not return until the middle of the week—if then.

I nearly swore aloud.

"Are they talking from the concierge's lodge or from the hotel? Burton, ask at both if they know the address of a Miss Sharp who brings bandages to the hospital!"

Of course by this time the connection had been cut off—and it took quite ten minutes to get on again—and by that time I could have yelled aloud with the feverish fret of it all, and the pain.

No one knew anything of a "Mees Shearp."

I mastered myself as well as I could and got into my chair.

And in a few moments Burton brought me a brandy and soda, and put it into my hand.

"It won't be cleared up enough to go back to Versailles before dinner, Sir Nicholas," he said— and coughed. "I was just thinking—maybe you'd be liking some friends to come and dine."

"Ask whom you please," I answered, and drank the brandy and soda down.

Presently, after half an hour, Burton came back to me, beaming.

He had telephoned the Ritz, and he had been informed that Mrs Bruce (Nina) had arrived the night before, alone—he had got connected up to her *appartement* and she would be round at eight o'clock, very pleased to dine!

Nina! A pleasant thrill ran through me— Nina, and without Jim!

The wood fire was burning brightly, and the curtains were drawn, when Nina, fresh as a rose, came in.

"Nicholas!" she cried delightedly, and held out both hands.

"Nina!—this is a pleasure, you old dear! Now let me look at you and see what marriage has done."

Nina drew back and laughed.

"Everything, Nicholas!" she said. "Why don't you marry, dear boy?"

"I would, but you forget, it would be from pity and not love that a woman would be kind to me."

"I am not quite sure of that, Nicholas," and she looked at me searchingly. "You are changed since last time. You are not so bitter and sardonic, and you always have that—'it.' Some kind of attraction that has no name, but I am sure has a lot to do with love."

"So you think I have got 'it,' Nina?"

"Yes, Nicholas, now that you are not so bitter—I am sure—but of course, you are in love!"

"And if so?"

"Who with?" she demanded.

"With a dream."

"Nonsense! You are much too cynical. Is it anyone I know?"

"I should not think so. She has not materialised yet."

"This is frightfully interesting, my dear old boy!"

"So you think I'll have a chance then?"

"Certainly, when you are all finished."

"My new eye is to be in at Christmas-time or sooner, and my new leg in a few weeks after—and my shoulder gets straighter every day!"

Nina laughed.

"Real love would be, I suppose, if you could make her adore you before you looked any handsomer!"

And this sentence of Nina's rang in my ears long after she had gone—and often in the night. I could not sleep—I felt that something had happened, and that fate might be going to take Miss Sharp—Alathea—away from me.

* * *

And then before morning in fretful dreams I seemed to be obsessed by the cooing of love words between a woman and a child.

* * *

Monday was a perfectly impossible day. I spent all the morning before I returned to Versailles in writing to Maurice, telling him he must find out all about Miss Sharp—Alathea.

Nina had suggested before she left that I should stay in Paris, and come to the theatre with her.

"We could have some delicious old times, Nicholas, now that you are so much better."

Once this would have thrilled me—only last spring! But now the contrariness in me made me say that it was absolutely necessary that I return immediately to Versailles.

I believe I should have answered like that even if there had been no Miss Sharp, Alathea, just because I now knew Nina really wanted me to stay; every man is like that, more or less, if only women knew!

Love, real love, is beyond all this. Love must be wonderful. I believe Alathea (I have actually written it naturally this time) could love.

But when I think of that scrap of a girl, with her elusive ways, her pride, her refinement, even her little red hands! I have a longing, a passionate longing, to hold her always near me, to know that she is mine, believing in her, respecting her.

Yes, that is it—*respecting her.* How few women one meets with attractions that one really respects.

How few are the women who have drawn

one's admiration or excited one's desire, and who at the same time one reverenced! Love must mean reverence—that is it.

I utterly reverence Alathea, and yet I am sure with that mouth if she loved me she would be anything but cold. How on God's earth can I make her love me?

I went back to Versailles after luncheon, having had to see the specialist about my eye; he now thinks that I could have the glass one in much sooner than Christmas. I wonder if some self-confidence will return when I can feel people are not revolted when looking at me?

When I get my leg, too, shall I have the nerve to make love to Alathea and use all the arts which used to be so successful in the old days?

I believe that if I were back in 1914 I should still be as nervous as a cat when with her. Is this one of the symptoms of love again?

I did not expect to hear anything of Alathea on the Monday, for she was not due until Tuesday at eleven o'clock; but when I came in from my sunset on the terrace, I found two telegrams. All the first one said was—

"EXTREMELY SORRY WILL BE UNABLE TO COME TOMORROW; BROTHER SERIOUSLY ILL.
                                        —A. SHARP."

And no address!

So I could not send sympathy—or even offer any help. I could have sworn aloud. The storm had wreaked its vengeance on someone then and the poor little chap had probably taken cold.

If I could only be of some use to them. Perhaps getting the best doctor is out of their reach.

I was full of turmoil while I tore open the other. This was from Suzette:

"I come this evening at eight."

It was nearly seven o'clock now, so I could not put her off, and I am not sure that I wanted to. Suzette is a human being and kindly, and her heart is warm.

When Burton was dressing me I told him of Miss Sharp's telegram.

"The poor young lady!" he said.

Burton always speaks of her as "the young lady." He never makes a mistake about class.

Suzette for him is "Mamzelle" and he speaks of her as a mother might about her boy's noisy, tiresome, rackety school friends—necessary evils, to be put up with for the boy's sake.

Nina he is politely respectful to, but to Miss Sharp he is absolutely reverential. She might be a Queen!

"I expect the poor little fellow got wet through, yesterday," I hazarded.

"He's that delicate," Burton remarked.

So Burton knows something more about the family than I do, after all!

"How did you know he was delicate, Burton? Or even that Miss Sharp had a brother?"

"I don't exactly know, Sir Nicholas—it's come out from one time to another—the young lady doesn't talk."

"How did you guess, then?"

"I've seen her anxious when I've brought in her tray—sometimes—and I once ventured to say to her, 'I beg pardon, Miss, but can I do anything for you?' and she took off her glasses suddenlike, and thanked me, and said it was her little brother she was worrying about.

"And you may believe me or not as you like, Sir Nicholas, but her eyes were full of tears."

I wonder if Burton understood the deep emotion he was causing me. My little darling!—with her beautiful blue eyes full of tears, and I impotent to comfort or help her!

"Yes—yes," I said.

"She told me then that he'd been delicate since birth, and she feared the winter in Paris for him—I do believe, Sir—it's that she works so hard for, to get him away south."

"Burton, what the devil can we do about it?"

"I don't very well know, Sir Nicholas. Many's the time I've badly wanted to offer her the peaches and grapes and other things, to take back to him; but of course I know my place better than to insult a lady."

He went on, now once started.

"I saw her outside a wine shop once when I got off the tram at Auteuil. She was looking at the bottles of port—and I made so as to pass, and her not see me, but she turned and said so friendly-like:

"'Burton, do you suppose this shop would keep really good port?'

"I said as how I would go in and see, and she came with me.

"Do you know, Sir, I could see she hadn't much with her—it was the day before she's paid, you see. Her colour came and went—then she said, 'I wonder, Burton, if you could oblige me with paying ten extra francs until tomorrow—I must have the best.'

"You may believe me, Sir Nicholas, I got out my purse quick enough—and then she thanked me so sweet like—'The doctor has ordered it for my mother, Burton,' she said, 'and of course she couldn't drink any but the best!' "

"Who on earth can she be, Burton? It does worry me—can't you possibly find out? I would so like to help them."

"I feel that, Sir—but here's the way I figure it. When gentry lives in foreign towns and don't seem anxious for you to know their address, it don't seem right like to pry into it."

"Burton, you dear old brick! Well, supposing we don't try to pry, but just try to see how we can possibly help her.

"You could certainly be sympathetic about the brother, since she has spoken to you—and surely something can be done? I saw her at the Duchesse's, you know—do you suppose she knows her?"

"I do, Sir Nicholas—I never meant to speak of it, but one day Her Grace came to see you and you were out and she caught sight of Miss Sharp through the half-open door."

"Then we should certainly be able to find out from the Duchesse?"

"Well, I would not be so sure of that, Sir Nicholas. You see, the Duchesse is a very kind lady, but she is a lady of the world, and she may have her reasons."

"Then what do you suggest, Burton?"

"Why, I hardly know—perhaps to wait and see, Sir Nicholas.

"It might be that I could do a bit of finding out if I felt sure no harm could come of it."

I was not quite certain what Burton meant by this. What possible harm could come of it?

"Find out all you can and let me know."

* * *

Suzette opened the door and came in just as I finished dressing. Burton left the room. She was pouting.

"So the book is not completed, Nicholas? And the English Mees comes three times a week?"

"Yes, does that upset you?"

"I should say!"

"May I not have a secretary? Next you will be objecting to my aunt coming to stay with me, or my dining with my friends!"

I was angry.

"No, *mon ami*—not that—they are not for me, those, but a secretary, a 'Mees'—*tiens!* For why do you want us two?"

"You *two?* Good Lord! Do you think, Suzette . . . ?

"You have overstepped the mark this time and there must be an end. Name whatever sum you want me to settle on you and then I don't ever wish to see you again."

She burst into frantic weeping. She had meant nothing! She was jealous! She loved me!

"Nonsense, Suzette! You have told me often it was only because I was very rich. Now be sensible, these things have to have an end someday. I shall be going back to England soon. So just let me make you comfortable and happy and let us part friends."

Finding the situation hopeless, Suzette accepted it, curbed the real emotion in herself, and played the game. She tried to amuse me, and then we discussed plans for her future. Then she said good-bye to me. She would go back to Paris by the last train.

"Good-bye, Suzette!" and I bent down and kissed her forehead. "You have been the jolliest little pal possible, and remember that I have appreciated it and you will always have a real friend in me!"

She burst into tears once more—real tears—and then she left me.

* * *

On Wednesday morning I received a reply from Maurice at Deauville—he hastened to answer, he said. He had heard of Miss Sharp through a man in the American Red Cross, where Miss Sharp had been employed. He knew nothing more about her.

I had tried to word my letter not to give the impression of peculiar interest, but he added that these people were often designing although they looked simple.

I would have been angry, only there was something humorous in the way people seem to think I am incapable of managing my own affairs!

Every one of my friends—and relations—would be hostile if I were to announce that I was in love with Miss Sharp and wanted to marry her —even though it was proved to them that she was pretty—a perfect lady—intelligent—virtuous—clever!

She is not of their set, and might, and probably would, be a stumbling-block in their path when they wished to make use of me.

None of them would put it in that way, of course; their opposition would be because they were thinking of *my* happiness!

Burton is the only person whose sympathy I could count upon.

How about the Duchesse?—That is the deepest mystery of all. I must find out from Burton what was the date about when she came to

my *appartement* and found Alathea. Was it before that time when she asked me if I was in love
—and I saw that dear little figure in the passage?

Could she have been thinking of her?

By Thursday when there was no further
news I began to feel so restless that I determined
to go back to Paris the following week. It was all
very well to be out in the *parc* at Versailles with
a mind at ease, but it feels too far away when
I am so troubled.

I sent Burton in on Friday to Auteuil.

"Just walk about near the wine shop, Burton, and try to find out, by every clue your not-
unintelligent old pate can invent, where Miss
Sharp lives, and what is happening.

"Then go to the Hotel de Courville and
chat with the concierge—or whoever you think
best—I simply can't stand hearing nothing!"

Burton pulled in his lips.

"Very good, Sir Nicholas."

I tried to correct my book in the afternoon.
I really am trying to do the things I feel she thinks
would improve my character. But I am one gnaw-
ing ache for news.

Monday. No news yet. It is unbearable. Burton returned from Auteuil with no clue whatso-
ever except that the concierge at the Hotel de
Courville had never heard of the name of Sharp.
That proves to me that "Sharp" is not Alathea's
name at all.

Nina turned up early on Saturday in time
for lunch.

We lunched in the restaurant. Some of the
Supreme War Council were about at the different

tables, and we exchanged a few words. Nina preferred it to my sitting-room.

"Englishmen do look attractive in uniform, Nicholas, don't they?" she said. "I wonder, if I had seen Jim in ordinary things, would I have been so drawn to him?"

"Who knows? Do you remember how sensible you were about him and Rochester? It is splendid that it has turned out so well."

"What is happiness, Nicholas?" and her eyes became dreamy.

Did she remember my words at our last meeting?

"Happiness is love and always to be satisfied with each other."

"What a fortunate woman she will be. And what else shall you give to her?"

"I shall give her passion, and tenderness, and protection, and devotion; she shall share the thoughts of my mind and the aspirations of my soul."

"Nicholas! You talking in this romantic way —she must be a miracle."

"No, she is just a little girl."

"And it is she who has made you think about souls?"

"I expect so."

And when the evening came and she left me, after our long day, I felt a sense of relief. Oh!—there can be no one in the world like my Alathea, with her little red hands, and cheap cotton garments!

I realise now that life used to be made up of the physical, and that something—perhaps suffering—has taught me that the mental and the spiritual matter more.

Even if she does come back, how am I to break through the wall of ice which she has surrounded herself with since the Suzette cheque business? I can't explain; she won't even know that I have parted with her.

Chapter
Six

Suspense is the hardest thing to bear. What a ridiculous truism! It has been said a thousand times before and will be said a thousand times again, because it has come to everyone at some moment, and so its pain is universally understood. I am filled with unrest.

I try to tell myself that Alathea Sharp does not matter in my life at all, that this is the end, that I am not to be influenced by her movements or her thoughts, or her comings and goings.

And then when I have succeeded in some measure in all this, a hideous feeling of sinking comes over me—that physical sensation of a lead weight below the heart. What on earth is the good of living an ugly, maimed life?

It was ten times easier to carry on under the most disgusting and fearsome circumstances when I was fighting than it is now when everything is done for my comfort and I have all that money can buy.

This evening it was wonderful on the terrace, the sun set in a blaze of crimson and purple and gold, every window in the Galerie des Glasses seemed to be on fire, and strange ghosts of bygone courtiers appeared to be flitting past the mirrors.

What do they think of the turmoil they have left behind them? I wonder. Is each generation torn by the same anguish which the worries of love bring?

But what is love anyway?—the thing itself, I mean. It is a want, and an ache, and a craving —I know what I want. I want firstly Alathea for my own, with everything which that term implies of possession.

Then I want to share her thoughts, and I want to feel all the great aspirations of her soul —and I want her companionship, I want her sympathy, I want her understanding.

When I was in love with Nina, and five or six others, I never thought of any of these things —I just wanted their bodies. Therefore, it is only when the spiritual enters into the damned thing, I suppose, that one could call it love.

By that reasoning, I have loved only Alathea in all my life. But I am stumped with this thought —if she had one eye and no leg below the knee, should I be in love with her, and feel all these exalted emotions about her?

I cannot honestly be certain how I would answer that question yet.

Until I can be quite sure that I should love Alathea just the same were she disfigured as I am, I cannot in justice expect her to return my passion.

I have done nothing to earn her respect. She has apprehended my useless life in these last months. And she knows that I have had a mistress. In heaven's name *why* should she be anything but what she is in her manner to me? Of course she despises me.

The only times I have ever seen any feeling at all in her for me were when she thought she had destroyed a wounded man's interest in a harmless hobby, and felt remorse.

And the freezing reserve which showed when she handed me the cheque-book, and the perturbation and contempt when I was rude about the child.

Now, what do I get out of the iciness over Suzette's cheque?

Two possibilities:

One, that she is more prudish than one of her literary cultivation and worldly knowledge is likely to be, so that she strongly disapproves of a man having a *petite amie,* or—

Two, that she has sensed that I love her, and was affronted at the discovery that at the same time I had a—friend.

The second possibility gives me hope, and so I fear to entertain a belief in it; but taken coldly it seems the most likely. Now, if she has *not* been affronted at this stage, would she have gone on believing I love her, and so eventually have shown some reciprocity?

It is just possible.

If only fate brings her to me again. Tomorrow it will be Monday—a whole week since I received her telegram.

I shall go up to Paris in the morning if I hear nothing and go myself to the Hotel de Courville to try and obtain a trace of her. If that is impossible, I will write to the Duchesse.

Reservoirs, Night

As I wrote the last words, a note was brought to me by Burton; someone had left it at the hotel.

Dear Sir Nicholas,

I am very sorry I have been unable to come out to do my work, but my brother died last Tuesday, and I have been extremely occupied. I will be at Versailles at eleven on Thursday as usual.

Yours truly,
A. Sharp

Her firm writing, more like a man's than a woman's, looked a little shaky at the end. Was she crying perhaps when she wrote the letter, the poor little girl? What will the death mean to her eventually? Will the necessity to work be lessened?

But even the gravity of the news did not prevent a feeling of joy and relief in me—I would see her again. Only four days to wait!

The weather has changed suddenly, the wind is sighing, and I know that the summer is over—I shall have the sitting-room fire lit and everything as comfortable as I can when she does turn up. I shall have to stay here until then since I cannot communicate with her in any way.

This ridiculous obscurity as to her address must be cleared away. I must try to ask her casually, so as not to offend her.

* * *

A week has passed.

Alathea came on Thursday. I was sickeningly nervous on Thursday morning. I was sitting in my chair quite still when the door opened, and in she came, just the scrap of a creature in dead black.

The black was supremely becoming to her transparent white skin, and seemed to set off the bright bronze brown of her hair. The irrepressible little curls had slipped out beside her ears, but the yellow horn spectacles were as uncompromising as ever.

I could not see whether her eyes were sad or no, but her mouth was firm as usual.

"I want to tell you of my sympathy," I said immediately. "I was so sorry not to know your address so that I might have expressed it to you before. I would have wished to send you some flowers."

"Thank you," was all she answered, but her voice trembled a little.

"It was so stupid of me not to have asked you for your address before. You must have thought it was so careless and unsympathetic."

"Oh, no!"

"Won't you give it to me now, so that I may know in the future?"

"We are going to move. It would be useless—it is not yet decided where we shall go."

I knew I dared not insist.

"Is there some place where I could be certain of a message reaching you, then? Because I would have asked you to come to the flat today and not out here if I could have found you."

She was silent for a moment. I could see she was in a corner. I felt an awful brute, but I had said it all quite naturally as would any employer who was quite unaware that there could be any reluctance to give the information.

I felt it was better to continue in this strain so as not to render her suspicious.

After a second or two she gave the number of a stationer's shop in the Avenue Mosart.

"I pass there every day," she said.

I thanked her.

"I hope you did not hurry back to your work —I can't bear to think that perhaps you would have wished to remain at home now."

"No, it does not matter."

There was an infinite weariness in her tone— a hopeless flatness I had never heard before; it moved me so that I blurted out—

"Oh! I have felt so anxious, and so sorry. I saw you in the Bois two Sundays ago in the thunderstorm, and I tried to get near the path I thought you would cross to offer you the carriage to return in, but I missed you. Perhaps your little brother caught cold there?"

There was a sob in her voice.

"Yes. Will you—would you—mind if we just did not speak of anything, but began work."

"Forgive me—I only want you to know that I'm so awfully sorry—and oh, if there was anything in the world I could do for you—would you not let me?"

"I appreciate your wish—it is kind of you —but there is nothing. You were going to begin the last chapter over again. Here is the old one —I will take off my hat while you look at it." She handed it to me.

Of course I could not say anything more. I had a big bunch of violets put on the table where she types, in Burton's room adjoining—they were the first forced ones which could be got in Paris —and I had slipped a card by them with just "My Sympathy" on it.

When she came back into the room, hatless, her cheeks were bright pink below the glasses— and all she said was "Thank you," and then I saw a little streak of wet trickle from under the horn rims.

I have never had such a temptation in my life—to stretch out my arms and cry, "Darling one, let me comfort you, here clasped close to me!" I longed to touch her—to express somehow that I felt profoundly for her grief.

"Miss Sharp," I did burst out, "I am not saying anything because I know you don't want me to—but it is not because I do not feel; I'm—I'm—awfully sorry. May not I perhaps send some roses to—your home—er—perhaps there is someone there who would like them."

"I'll take the violets with me, if you will let me," she said. "Please don't trouble about anything more—and do let us begin work."

So we started upon the chapter.

Her hands were not so red, I noticed. I am becoming sensitive to what is called "atmosphere," I suppose.

I was aware that my natural emotions were running riot, and that my one eye was gazing at her with love in it, and that my imagination was conjuring up scenes of delight with her as a companion.

Her want of complete control allowed the waves to reach her, I expect—for I knew that she was using all her will to keep her attention upon the work, and that she was nearly as disturbed as I was myself.

But how was she disturbed? Was she just nervous from events—or was I causing her any personal trouble?

The moment I felt that perhaps I was, a feeling of assurance and triumph came over me!

I *knew* that she was giving way and talking with less stiffness because she was weak with sorrow and probably had not had much sleep. I *knew* that it was not because she had forgotten about the Suzette cheque or really was more friendly.

I *knew* that I was taking an unfair advantage of her—but I continued—men are really brutes, after all—and gloried in my power every time the slightest indication showed that I possessed it! I lost some of my diffidence.

If only I could have stood upon two feet and seen with two eyes—I know that even the morning would have ended by my taking her in my arms, cost what might.

But as I was glued to my chair, she was enabled always at this stage to stay out of reach, and fenced gallantly with me by silence and stiff answers.

But by luncheon time there was a distinct gain on my side—I had made her feel something; I no longer was a nonentity who did not count.

Her skin is so transparent that the colour fluctuates with every emotion. I love to watch it. What a mercy that I had very strong sight, for my one eye sees quite clearly!

At luncheon we talked of many things. Alathea is so wonderfully well read.

"You are not thinking of leaving Paris, I hope, when you move," I said, as we drank coffee. "I am going to begin another book directly this one is finished."

"It is not yet decided," she answered abruptly.

"I could not write without you."

Silence.

"I would love to think that you took an interest in teaching me how to be an author."

The faintest shrug of the shoulders.

"You don't take any interest?"

"No."

"Why?"

"Are you not very unkind?"

"No. If you have anything to complain of in my work, I will listen attentively and try to alter it."

"You will never allow the slightest friendship?"

"No."

"Why?"

"Why should I?"

"I must be grateful even that you ask a question, I suppose. Well, I don't myself know quite why you should. You think I am a rotter—you despise my character—you think my life is wasted, and that—er—I have undesirable friends."

Silence. I was stung to exasperation.

"Miss Sharp! You drive me crazy, never answering—I can't think why you like to be so provoking!"

"Sir Nicholas"—and she put down her cup, with displeasure—"if you will not keep to the subject of work, I am sorry, but I cannot stay as your secretary."

Terror seized me.

"I shall have to if you insist upon it, I suppose; but I am longing to be friends with you, and I can't think why you should resent it so. We are both English, we are both—unhappy—and we are both lonely."

Silence!

"Somehow I don't feel it is altogether because I am a revolting object to look at that you are so unkind—you must have seen lots like me since the war."

"I am not unkind, but I think you are. May I go to my work now?"

We rose from the table and for a second she was so near to me that the pent-up desire of weeks mastered me, and the tantalization of the morning overcame me, so that a frantic temptation seized me—I *could not* resist it.

I put out one arm while I steadied myself with the other by the back of a chair, and I drew her tiny body towards me, and pressed my lips to her Cupid's bow of a mouth, and oh, God, the pleasure of it—right or wrong!

She went dead white. When I released her she trembled, and in her turn held on to the back of the chair.

"How dare you!" she panted. "How dare you! . . . I will go this minute. You are not a gentleman."

The reaction came to me.

"That is it, I suppose," I said hoarsely—"I am not a gentleman underneath—the civilisation is mere veneer—and the *man* breaks through it. You will have to weigh up as to whether it is worth your while to stay with me or not.

"I can only assure you that I will try not to err again. I shall go to my room now, and you can let me have your decision in an hour or so."

I could not move because my crutch had fallen to the floor, out of my reach. She stood in indecision for a moment, and then she bent and picked it up and gave it to me. She was still as white as a ghost. As I got to the door I turned and said—

"I apologise for having lost my self-control —I am ashamed of that—and do not ask you to forgive me. Your staying or not is a business arrangement. I give you my word I will try never to be so weak again."

I bowed and hobbled on into my bedroom, shutting the door after me.

Here my courage deserted me. I got to the bed with difficulty and threw myself down upon it and lay there, too filled with emotion to stir. The thought tormented me always. Have I burnt my boats—or is this only the beginning of a new stage?

Time will tell.

* * *

I lay and wondered and wondered what were Alathea's emotions after I left her. Should I ever know? When the hour was up I went back into the sitting-room. I had struggled against the awful depression which was overcoming me.

If my insult had been deliberate or planned, I would have held her longer, and knowing I was going to lose her by my action, I would have profited by it.

The only thing I was glad about was that I had not attempted to ask forgiveness. If I had done so, she would undoubtedly have walked straight out of the hotel; but having just had the sense to leave her to think for a while—perhaps—?

Well, I was sitting in my chair, feeling some kind of numb anguish which I suppose those going to be hanged experience. When Burton brought in my tea and I heard no sound of clicking next door, I asked him as naturally as I could if Miss Sharp had gone.

"Yes, Sir Nicholas," he answered, and the shock, even though it was expected, was so great that for a second I closed my eye.

She had left a note, he further added, putting the envelope down on the table beside the tray.

I made myself light a cigarette and not open it, and I made myself say casually:

"I am afraid she feels her brother's death dreadfully, Burton!"

"The poor young lady, Sir Nicholas! She must have kept up brave-like all the time this morning, and then after lunch while you were resting, Sir, it got too much for her, I expect, sitting alone—for she was sobbing like to break her heart as I opened the door.

"She looked so forlorn and huddled up—give you my word, Sir Nicholas, I was near crying myself."

"I am so awfully sorry. What did you do, Burton?"

"I said: 'Let me bring you a nice cup of tea, Miss.' It is always best to bring ladies tea when they are upset, Sir Nicholas, as you may know.

"She thanked me sweet-like, as she always does; and I made so bold as to say how sorry I was, and I did hope she had not had any extra trouble to deal with over it; and how I'd be so glad to advance her her next week's salary if it would be any convenience to her—knowing funerals and doctors are expensive.

"Out of my own money, of course, I gave her to understand—because I knew she be bound to refuse yours, Sir Nicholas. . . . At that her tears burst out afresh. She had no glasses on, and she looked no more than sixteen years old.

"Give you my word, Sir. She thanked me as if it was something really kind I'd thought of.

"Then she seemed to be having a struggle with herself—just as if she'd rather die than take anything from anybody—and yet knew she had to. She turned them blue eyes on me, streaming with tears, and I had to turn away, Sir Nicholas.

" 'Burton,' she says, 'have you ever felt that you wanted to be dead and done with it all—that you couldn't fight any more?'

" 'I can't say as I have, Miss,' I answered her—'but I know my master feels that way often.' Perhaps she felt kinder sorry for you too, Sir Nicholas, because as I said that, she gave a sort of extra-sharp sob and buried her face in her hands.

"I slipped out of the room then and brought the tea as quick as I could, you may believe me, Sir, and by that time she had pulled herself together.

" 'It is stupid to have any proud feelings if you have to work, Burton,' she said. 'I will be ... grateful for the loan of your money, and I am happy to have such a friend' . . . She put out her little bit of hand, she did, Sir Nicholas, and I never felt so proud in my life.

"When I came back for the tray she had her hat on, and the note written for you, Sir. I took the violets and began putting them in the box for her to take, but she stopped me.

" 'Violets fade so soon, I will not take them, thank you,' she said."

I could not answer Burton. I just nodded my head and the dear old boy left me alone. My very heart seemed bursting with pain and remorse. When he had gone I seized the letter and opened it.

To Sir Nicholas Thormonde, Bart., V.C.

Dear Sir,

Circumstances force me to work, so I shall have to remain in your service, if you require me. I am unfortunately quite defenceless, so I appeal to whatever chivalry

there is in you not to make it so impossible
that I must again give in my resignation.
                        Yours faithfully,
                            A. *Sharp*

I fell back in my chair in an agony of emotion. To have had to write such a letter—to me!
    The unspeakable brute I felt!
    For the rest of the day and night I suffered
every shade of self-reproach and abasement a man
can feel. And next day I had to stay in bed because I had done some stupid thing to my shoulder in lying down without help.
    When I knew I could not get into Paris by
Saturday when Alathea was to come to the flat, I
sent Burton in with a note to the wine shop in
the Avenue Mosart.

> Dear Miss Sharp,
>   I am deeply grateful for your magna-
> nimity and I am utterly ashamed of my weak-
> ness—and you will not have called upon my
> chivalry in vain, I promise you. I have to stay
> in bed, so I cannot be at the flat, and if you
> receive this in time I shall be obliged if you
> will come out here again, on Saturday.
>   Yours very truly,
>   *Nicholas Thormonde*

Then I never slept all night, with thoughts of
longing and wondering if she would get it soon
enough to come.
    Over and over in my vision I saw the picture
of her sitting there in Burton's room, sobbing. My
action was the last straw—my shameful action—
Burton showed the good taste and the sympathy
and understanding for her which I should have
done.

And to think that she is troubled about money, so that she had to take a loan from my dear old servitor—far greater gentleman than I am.

I can go on no longer in this anguish—as soon as I feel that peace is in the smallest measure restored between us—I will ask her to marry me, just so that I can give her everything.

I shall tell her that I expect nothing from her—only the right to help her family and give her prosperity and peace.

Sunday. I was still in bed on Saturday morning at eleven. The doctor came out to see me very early, and insisted that I be kept quite still until Monday. So Burton had my bed table brought, and all my papers and things.

There had come a number of letters to answer, and he had asked me if Miss Sharp could not do them as soon as she arrived.

"Burton, perhaps she'll feel not quite at ease with me alone in here like this. Could you not make some excuse to be tidying drawers and stay while I am dictating," I said.

"Very good, Sir Nicholas."

When he replies with those words I know that he is agreeing—but with reservations.

"Out with what you are thinking, Burton."

"Well, Sir Nicholas"—and he coughed—"Miss Sharp—is so understanding that she'd know in a minute that you'd got me there on purpose. It might make her awkward-like."

"You may be right; we will see how things turn out."

Presently I heard Alathea in the sitting-room and Burton went in to see her.

"Sir Nicholas is very poorly today, Miss," I

heard him say. "The doctor won't let him out of bed. I wonder if you'd be so kind as to take down his letters—they are too much for him himself, not being able to sit up, and I have not the time."

"Of course I will, Burton," her soft voice answered.

"I've put the table and everything ready, and I thank you kindly," Burton went on. "I am glad to see you looking better, Miss."

I listened intently. It seemed as if I could hear her taking off her hat, and then she came into the room to me; but by that time my heart was beating so rapidly I could not speak loud.

I said "good-morning" in some half-voice, and she answered the same, then she came forward to the table. Her dear little face was very pale and there was something pathetic in the droop of her lips. Her hands, I noticed, were again not so red.

"All the letters are there." I pointed to the pile. "It will be so good of you if you will do them now."

She took each one up and handed it to me without speaking and I dictated the answer. I had had one from Suzette that morning, but I was clearly under the impression that I had put it with one from Maurice on the other side of the bed, so I had no anxiety about it.

Then suddenly I saw Alathea's cheeks flame crimson and her mouth shut with a snap—and I realised that the irony of fate had fallen upon me again, for she had picked up Suzette's lavender-tinted, highly scented missive.

She handed it to me without a word.

The letter ended:

Adieu, Nicholas! pour toujours!
Tu es Mon Adore,
Ta Suzette

But the way it was folded only showed "Tu es Mon Adore" and "Ta Suzette"—and this much Alathea had certainly seen.

I felt as if there were some evil imp laughing in the room. There was nothing to be said or done. I could not curse aloud—so I simply took the letter, and indicated that I was waiting for the next one to be handed to me.

So Alathea continued her work. But could anything be more maddening—more damnably provoking!—and more inopportune? Why must the shadow of Suzette fall upon me all the time?

This of course will make any renewal of even the coldest friendliness impossible between my little girl and me. I cannot ask her to marry me now, and perhaps not for a long time, if ever the chance comes to me again, in any case.

Her attitude, carriage of head, and expression of mouth showed contempt as she finished the shorthand notes—and then she rose and went into the other room to type, closing the door after her.

And I lay there shivering with rage and chagrin.

I saw no more of Alathea that morning. She had her lunch in the sitting-room alone, and Burton brought the dishes in to me, and after lunch he insisted that I should sleep for an hour until half past two o'clock. He had some accounts for Miss Sharp to do, he said.

I was so exhausted that when I did fall asleep I slept until nearly four—and awoke with a start, and an agony of apprehension that she might have gone; but no—Burton said she was still there when I rang for him, and I asked him to have her come to me again.

We went over one of the earlier chapters in the book and I made some alterations in it; she never showed the slightest interest, nor did she speak.

Tea came in for us both. She poured it out, still without uttering a word—she remembered my taste of no sugar or milk, and put the cup near me so that I could reach it.

She handed me the plate of those nasty make-believe biscuits which is all we can get now —then she drank her own tea.

The atmosphere had grown so tense that it was supremely uncomfortable. I felt that I must break the ice.

"How I wish there were a piano here!" I remarked, apropos of nothing—and of course she greeted this with her usual silence.

"I am feeling so rotten, and if I could hear some music it would make me better."

She made the faintest movement with her head—to show me, I suppose, that she was listening respectfully but saw no occasion to reply.

I felt so unspeakably wretched and helpless and useless lying there, I had not the pluck to go on trying to talk, so I closed my eye and lay still, and then I heard Alathea rise and go softly towards the door.

"I will type this at home, and return it to the flat on Tuesday, if that will be all right," she said; and I answered—

"Thank you," and turned my face to the wall.

And now I am in much better health again, and Maurice is coming to dine with me.

Chapter
Seven

I was awfully glad to see old Maurice again —he was looking brown and well. He congratulated me on the improvement in health in myself too, and then he gave me all the news.

The war was simply growing into a nuisance, and the quicker it was over the better for everyone.

Then he beat about the bush for a little longer, and at last began to grow nearer the vital subject, and finally plunged in—

"You are not—becoming entangled in any way with your secretary, are you, *mon ami?*" he asked.

I had decided beforehand that I would not get angry at anything he said—so I was ready for this.

"No, Maurice," and I poured out a second glass of port for him. Burton had left us alone by now.

"Miss Sharp does not know that I exist—she is simply here to do her work, and is the best secretary any man could want."

Maurice sipped his port. "I heard you were interested."

I remained undisturbed.

"I am immensely interested. I want to know who she really is. She is a lady, even a lady of our world. I mean, she knows about things in England, where she has never been—things that she could not possibly know unless her family had spoken of them always.

"Can't you find anything out for me, old boy, as to who she is?"

"I will certainly try. Sharp? It is not a name of the *haut monde*—no?"

"Of course that is not her real name."

"Why don't you ask her yourself, *mon brave?*"

"I'd like to find a man with pluck enough to ask her anything she did not wish him to!"

"That little girl! But she appeared meek and plain, and respectable, Nicholas. You intrigue me!"

"Well, put your wits to work, Maurice, and promise me you will not talk to the others about anything. I shall be very angry if you do."

He gave me every assurance he would be silent as the grave—and then he changed the topic to that of Suzette. He was sorry I had given her her *congé*.

I told him I had absolutely finished with that part of my life—I loathed the whole idea of it now.

Maurice inspected me with grave concern.

"My dear chap—this appears serious. You are not *in love* with your secretary, are you?—or is it possible that you are bluffing, and that she has replaced Suzette?"

I felt a hot flush mounting to my forehead.

But Maurice meant no personal disrespect to Alathea. For him, women were either of the world, or they were not.

"Look here, Maurice, I want you to understand that Miss Sharp is a lady in every way—I have already told you this, but you don't seem to have grasped it—and that she has my greatest respect—and it makes me sick to think of anyone talking of her as you have just done."

"Your interest is then serious, Nicholas?"

Maurice was absolutely aghast!

"My *respect* is serious—my curiosity is hot—and I want information."

Maurice promised that he would try—and our talk turned to the Duchesse—he had seen her at a cross-country station as he came up, and she would be back in Paris the following week. This thought gave me comfort.

Everyone would be back by the fifteenth of October, he assured me, and then we could all amuse ourselves again.

"You will be quite well enough to dine out, Nicholas—or if not you must move to the Ritz with me so that you at least have entertainment on the spot, *mon cher!*"

When he had left me I lay back in my chair and asked myself what had happened to me, that Maurice and his friends seemed such miles and miles away from me.

How I must have sunk during the years. Surely even a one-eyed, one-legged man ought to be able to do something for his country politically, it suddenly seemed to me—and what a glorious picture to gaze at!

If I could someday go into Parliament and have Alathea beside me, to give me inspiration, and help me to achieve the best in myself . . .

And I dreamed and dreamed in the firelight —things all filled with sentiment and exaltation.

How I would love to have Alathea for my wife —and have children. It can't be possible that I

have written that! I loathe children in the abstract
—they bore me to death. But to have a son—
with Alathea's eyes—God!—how the thought
makes me feel!

And now what have I to face?

A will stronger than or as strong as my own.
A prejudice of the deepest which I cannot explain
away.

A knowledge that I have no power to retain
the thing I love, nothing but the material thing of
money, which, because of her great unselfishness
and desire to benefit her loved ones, she might
be forced to consider.

My only possibility of obtaining her at all is
to buy her with money. And once bought—when
I had her here in my house—would I have the
strength to resist the temptation to take advantage
of the situation?

Could I go on day after day never touch-
ing her—never having any joys—until the great-
ness of my love somehow melted her dislike and
contempt of me?

I wish to God I knew.

She will never marry me unless I give my
word of honour that the thing will only be an
empty ceremony—of that I feel sure, even if circumstances aid me to force her into doing this
much.

And then one has to keep one's word of
honour. And might not that be a greater hell of
suffering than I am now in?

Perhaps I had better go to the sea and try
to break the whole chain and forget her.

I rang the bell for Burton then, and told him
of my new plan as he put me to bed. We would
go off to Saint-Malo for a week.

I wrote to Alathea without weakening. I

asked her to collect the manuscript, and during my absence make notes of what she thought still should be altered.

I wrote as stiffly and in as business-like a manner as possible—and finally I went to sleep, and slept better than I have done for some time.

* * *

Saint-Malo

How quaint these places are! I am at this deserted corner by the sea where the hotel is comfortable and hardly touched by the war. I am not happy—the air is doing me good, that is all.

I tell myself continually that I am no more interested in Alathea—that I am going to get well and go back to England. That I have emerged, and am a man with a free will once more, and I am a great deal better.

After all, how absurd to be thinking of a woman from morning to night!

When I get my new leg and everything is all healed up, in a year or two, shall I be able to ride again? Of course I shall, no doubt—and even play a little tennis?

Yes, of course life is a gorgeous thing. I like the fierce wind to blow in my face—and yesterday, much to Burton's displeasure, I went out sailing.

* * *

A week has passed since we came to this end of the earth—and again I have grown restless—perhaps it is because Burton came in just now with a letter in his hand. I recognised immediately Alathea's writing.

"I made so bold as to leave the young lady our address before we left, Sir Nicholas, in case she wanted to communicate with us, and she writes now to say, would I be good enough to ask you if you took with you chapter seven, because she cannot find it anywhere."

Then he went on with evident constraint to tell me that the rest of the letter said that while she was working on Friday, a "Mademoiselle la Blonde" called, and insisted upon passing Pierre, who answered the door, and coming in to her— "It was Mamzelle, of course, Sir Nicholas!" Burton snapped.

She had demanded my address, but Miss Sharp had not felt she was justified in giving it to her—but had said letters would be forwarded.

"I hope to goodness that the baggage made no scene with the young lady, Sir Nicholas," Burton growled.

"Nor I either," I retorted angrily. "Suzette ought to know better, now that I have given her everything she wanted. Will you let her understand, please, that this must not occur again?"

So here was a fresh barrier arisen between Alathea and myself!—a fresh barrier which I cannot explain away.

The only comfort I get out of the whole thing is that imperative necessity must have been driving my little darling—or she would not put up with any of these things for a moment.

If money is so necessary to her—perhaps after all I could get her to consent to marry me. The very thought made my pulses bound again—and all my calm flew to the winds.

I knew that once more I was as utterly under the spell of her attraction as I had been the moment when my passionate lips touched her soft reluctant ones.

I spent the rest of the day dreaming about

the joy of that kiss, until by night-time I was as mad as a hatter and more full of cruel unrest than ever.

I hate this place—I hate the sea. It is all of no use—I shall go back to Paris.

* * *

The first thing I learned when I reached the *appartement* was that the Duchesse had returned, and wished to see me. This was good news—and without even telephoning to Maurice, I got into my one-horse Victoria and repaired to the Hotel de Courville.

The Duchesse was sitting in her boudoir upstairs when I got in. She had a quaint expression upon her face. I was not certain that her greeting was as cordial as usual. Has gossip reached her ears also?

I thought I would begin at once, before she could say anything which might make questioning her impossible.

"I have been longing to see you, Duchesse, to ask you if you could help me to find out who my secretary, Miss Sharp, is. Because I saw her here in the passage one day, and I thought you might possibly be able to identify her—"

"*Tiens?*"

"Her Christian name is 'Alathea'—I heard her little sister call her that once when I saw them and they did not see me, in the Bois. She is a lady—and I feel 'Sharp' is not her name at all."

The Duchesse put on her eyeglasses.

"She has not shown a sign that she wishes you to know her history?"

"No."

"Then, my son, do you think it is very good taste to endeavour to discover it?"

"Perhaps not." I was nettled—I hated that the Duchesse should be displeased with me—nevertheless, I then went on: "I fear that she is very poor, and I know that her little brother died just lately, and I would give anything in the world to help them in some way."

"Sometimes one helps more by showing discretion."

"You won't assist me in any way then, Duchesse? I *feel* that you know Miss Sharp."

She frowned.

"Nicholas—if I did not love you really, I should be angry. Am I of the character to betray friends—presuming that I have friends—for a young man's curiosity?"

"Indeed, it is not curiosity, it is because I want to help."

"Camouflage!"

I felt angry now.

"You assume that your secretary is a *demoiselle du monde*," she went on. "If you have reached that far, you should know that there is some honour left in old families, and so you should treat her with consideration, and respect her incognito. All this is not like you, my son!"

"I want to treat her with every respect," I reiterated.

"Then, believe me, it is unnecessary for you to know her name. I am not altogether pleased with you, Nicholas."

"Dear Duchesse! That grieves me. I wish I could explain—I have only wanted to be kind—and I don't even know her address and could not send flowers when her brother died."

"They did not want flowers, perhaps. Take my advice—of the best I can give. Pay your secretary her wages—as high a wage as she will accept—and then treat her as if she were fifty years old—and wore glasses!"

"She does wear glasses—abominable yellow horn-rimmed spectacles," I announced excitedly. "Have you never seen them?"

The Duchesse's eyes flashed.

"I have not said I have ever met Miss Sharp, Nicholas."

I knew the affair was now hopeless—and that I would only risk the real displeasure of my dear old friend if I continued in this way. So I subsided. I had some instinct, too, that I would not receive sympathy even if I owned that my intentions were strictly honourable!

"I will say no more—except that should you know these people, *chère* Duchesse, and should you ever discover that I could help them in any way, you will call upon me to any extent."

She looked at me very searchingly and said laconically—

"*Bien.*"

Then we talked of other things, and I tried to reingratiate myself. The war was going better. When was I going to England?

"When I am out of the hands of these doctors, and have my new leg and eye—I will return, and then I want to go into Parliament."

The Duchesse warmed up at once. That was just the thing for me to do—that, and to marry some nice girl of my own world.

"I would want such an exceptional woman, Duchesse."

"Do not look for the moon, my son."

"Do you think a woman ought to be perfectly innocent and ignorant of life to make marriage happy?" I asked. "Duchesse, I want someone who would love me passionately, and whom I could passionately love."

"For that, my poor boy"—and she sighed—"it is not found among young girls. Love! *Mon Dieu*, it is the song of poets, it cannot happen in the world—with satisfaction."

"There is no hope of my finding someone I could really love, then?"

"I do not know—in your country, it may be."

"But, Duchesse—with your great heart—have you never loved?"

Her eyes seemed to grow beautiful and young again—they diffused a fiery light.

"Loved! Nicholas, all women love once in their lives—happy for them if it has not burnt their souls in its passage. Happy if the *bon Dieu* has let it merge into love for humanity." And soft tears dimmed the dark blue brilliancy.

I leaned forward and kissed her hand with deep devotion—then the ancient servitor came in and she was called to a ward.

But I left feeling that if there is really some barrier of family between Alathea and myself, there would be no use in my appealing to the Duchesse.

The only thing left now was to telephone to Maurice.

He came in for a few minutes just before dinner.

He had again questioned Alwood Chester of the American Red Cross, who had told him that Miss Sharp had been Miss Sharp always while she worked for them, and that no one knew anything further about her.

Well, if her father is a convict, and her mother in a mad-house, and her sister consumptive—I still want her for herself.

Is that true? Could I face disease and insanity coming into my family?

I don't know. All I know is that whatever curse hangs over the rest, I do not believe it has touched her. She is the picture of health and balance and truth. Her every action is noble—and I love her—I love her.

Next day she came in at ten as usual. As her attitude towards me has been as cold as it was possible for an attitude to be, I cannot say that there was any added shade of contempt since her interview with Suzette.

What had passed between them perhaps Burton will be able gradually to discover.

I controlled myself, and behaved with a business-like reserve. She had nothing to snub me for and did not seem to be disturbed. She took the papers at twelve o'clock—and I sighed as she left the room. I had watched her furtively for nearly two hours.

Her hands are whitening considerably. I believe their redness had something to do with her little brother—perhaps she put very hot things on his chest. I have never seen such a white skin—it shows like mother-of-pearl against the cheap black frock.

The line of her throat is like that of my fascinating Nymph with the shell—indeed, her mouth is not unlike hers also. I wonder if she has dimp— But I had better not think of those things!

I am now determined to ask her to marry me on the first occasion I can screw up my courage sufficiently. I have decided what I am going to say. I am going to be quite matter-of-fact—I shan't tell her that I love her even—I feel if I can secure her first, I shall have a better chance afterwards. If she thought I loved her, her nature is of

that honest kind that she might think it was dis-
honourable to make so uneven a bargain with me;
but if she thinks I want her just for my secretary
and to play to me—she may feel that it is fair for
her to take my name, and my money.

And give me nothing in return.

I had better accept the shadow of Suzette
falling upon my relation with Alathea, and try to
gain my end in spite of it. And what is my very
end?

Not of course that I shall spend the rest of
my life as Alathea's "husband-in-name-only,"
hungry and longing and miserable—but that after securing her certain companionship I shall
overcome her prejudices, conquer her aversion,
and make her love me.

But to have the chance to do all of this it is
absolutely necessary that I be near her always. So
my idea of marriage is not so far-fetched after
all!

And if she will accept me, someday, upon
any terms—provided that they do not mean sep-
aration—I shall believe that half the battle is won;
I feel more cheerful already!

* * *

Burton gave forth some information this
evening, as he was dressing me for dinner. He had
now discovered from Pierre how Suzette had
behaved when she intruded upon Alathea.

She had entered the room—"passing Pierre
without so much as asking his leave, and he with
his wooden leg not so nimble as might be." She
had gone up to the writing-table and demanded
my address. "An affair of business which must be
attended to at once," she had announced.

Pierre, standing at the door, had heard all of this.

Alathea apparently had answered, with dignity, that she had received no orders to give any address, but that letters would be forwarded.

"She took no more notice of Mamzelle than if she was a chair," Pierre had told him. Suzette became nonplussed, and losing her temper a little told Alathea that she hoped she would get as much out of the situation as she herself had done!

Alathea continued writing as though she had not heard, and then told her quite politely, in French, that if she would kindly leave whatever letters were to be sent on, she would see that they went that night, and added—

"Now, I need not detain you longer."

Suzette became furious, and stamping, said she was Mademoiselle la Blonde, and had more right there than Alathea had!

Pierre here interfered, and catching hold of Suzette's arm, had dragged her from the room.

I tingled with shame and wrath. That the person I respect most in the world should have been exposed to such a scene! ... Burton too was horrified. ...

I had the most awful sensation of discomfort —the very fact of having to hear all this through servants was sufficiently disgusting, without the events themselves being so degrading.

What must Alathea think of me! And I cannot even allude to the subject. How wonderful her dignity has been, that she has allowed no extra contempt to come into her manner.

How shall I have the pluck to ask her to marry me? I mean to do so tomorrow when she comes.

Saturday. I am going to write the events of these last days down without any comment.

I came into the sitting-room after Alathea had arrived. She was writing at her desk in the little Salon. I looked in and asked her if she would come and speak to me. Then I got to my chair. She entered obediently, with the block in her hand, ready to begin work.

"Will you sit down, please," I said, indicating a chair where she would face me and the light, so that no shade of her expression should be lost upon me.

I felt less nervous than I had ever before felt when with her. I thought there was the faintest shade of alertness in her manner.

"I am going to say something which will surprise you very much, Miss Sharp," I began.

She raised her head a little.

"I will put the case to you quite baldly. I am very rich, as you know—I am still quite horrid to look at—I am lonely, and I want a companion who would play the piano to me and who would help me to write books, and travel with me.

"I cannot have any of these simple things because of the scandal people would make, so there is only one course open to me, and that is to go through the marriage ceremony. Miss Sharp —under those terms, will you marry me?"

Her attitude had become tense; her face did not flush, instead it became very pale. She remained perfectly silent for a moment. I felt just the same as I used to do before going into battle— a queer kind of excitement—a wonder if I'd come through or not.

As she did not answer, I went on: "I would not expect anything from you except a certain amount of your company. There would not be any

question of your living with me as a wife—I would
promise even to keep in check that side which
you once saw, and which I was so sorry about.

"I would settle lots of money on you, and
give anything to your family you might wish. I
would not bother you, you would be quite free
—only I would like you to take interest in my
work, in a way, and to play to me, even if you
would not talk to me."

My voice broke a little at the end of this; I
was conscious of it, and of how weak it was of
me. Her hands clasped together suddenly and
she appeared as though she was going to speak,
then remained silent.

"Won't you answer me at all?" I pleaded.

"It is such a strange proposal—I would
wish to refuse it at once . . ."

"It is quite bald, I know," I interrupted quickly. "I want to buy you—that is all; you can name
the price. I know if you consented it would
merely be for the same reason which makes you
work.

"I presume it is for your family, not for yourself; therefore, I am counting upon that to in-
fluence you. Whatever you would want for your
family I should be delighted to give you."

She twisted her locked hands—the first sign
of real emotion I have seen in her.

"You would marry me without knowing anything about me? It is very strange. . . ."

"Yes—I think you are extremely intelligent
—if you would consent to talk to me sometimes.
I want to go into Parliament when I am patched
up and more decent-looking, and I believe you
would be of the greatest help to me."

"You mean the whole thing simply as a business arrangement?"

"I have already stated that."

She started to her feet.

"The bargain," I went on, "would be quite a fair one. I am offering to buy a thing which is not for sale—therefore, I am willing to pay whatever would tempt the owner to part with it. I am not mixing up any sentiment in the affair."

Her lips were quivering.

"You would say this no matter what you might hear of my family?"

"I am quite unconcerned as to their history. I have observed you, and you possess all the qualities which I want in the partner who can help me to live my new life. For me you are just a personality"—thus I lied valiantly!—"not a woman."

"Can I believe you?" she asked a little breathlessly.

"You are thinking of that day when I kissed you." Her lips told me by their sudden drawing in that she was agitated.

"Well—I expect really that you know men well enough, Miss Sharp, to know that they have sudden temptations—but that a strong will can overcome them.

"If you will marry me, I will give you my word I will never touch you, or expect anything of you, except what you agree to give in the bargain. You can lead your own life—and I can lead mine."

I felt suddenly that these last words were not very wise—for they aroused in her mind the thought that I should go on having friends like Suzette. I hastened to add—

"You will have my deepest respect, and as my wife shall be treated with every courtesy and honour."

She sat down again and raised her hands to her eyes as though to remove her glasses, and then remembered and dropped them.

"I see that you would rather not answer to-day, Miss Sharp—you might prefer to go now and think about it?"

"Thank you." She turned and walked back into the little Salon without a word more, and when she went I closed my eye, exhausted with the great strain.

But I did not feel altogether hopeless—until Burton came in to tell me lunch was ready and said that Alathea had gone.

"The young lady said as how she expected she would not be back, and she took her own pens and things in her bag; she was as white as a lily, I give you my word, Sir Nicholas."

I am ashamed to say that I felt a little faint then. Had I overstepped the mark, and should I never see her again?

Burton gave me a sleeping draught that night, and I slept far into the next day, to awake more unhappy than ever.

In the afternoon I received a note from Maurice, telling me that he had inadvertently heard that a fellow in the American Red Cross had seen Miss Sharp's passport, when she had been sent down to Brest for them, and the name on it was Alathea Bulteel Sharp.

And, judging that the second name sounded as if it might be a well-known English one, he hastened to tell me, in case it should be a clue.

I could not think where I had heard it before lately, or what memory it was connecting in my brain.

I had a feeling it was something to do with a friend of mine, George Harcourt. I puzzled for a while, and then I looked back over the pages of my journal, and there found what I had written of some of his conversation—

Bobby Bulteel—the Hartelfords' brother—cheating at cards—and married to Lady Hilda Marchant . . .

Of course! . . . The whole thing became plain to me. This would account for everything. I hobbled up and got down the *Peerage*. I turned to the Hartelford title, and noted the brothers—the Hon'bles—John Sinclair, Charles Henry, and Robert Edgar—this last must be "Bobby."

Then I read the usual thing—"Educated at Eton and Christchurch," etc., etc.; "formerly Captain the —— Guards.

"Married in 1894—Lady Hilda Farwell, only daughter of the Marquis of Braxted (title extinct) and divorced wife of William Marchant, Esquire.

"Issues—Alathea, born 1894—John Robert, born 1905—and Hilda, born 1907 . . ."

So the whole tragic story seemed to unfold itself before me. . . .

Alathea was the child of that great love and sacrifice of her mother—I read again the words George had used: "She adored the fellow, who had every charm. All the world might cast him out, but that one faithful woman gave up home and name and honour to follow him in his disgrace.

"That was love indeed, however misplaced!"

I looked again at the dates and made a calculation—of the time divorces took—and I saw that my little darling girl could only have escaped illegitimacy by perhaps a few hours!

What had Alathea's life been? I pictured it. They must have hidden in hole-and-corner places during the dreary years. The Hartelfords were poor as church mice, and were not likely to assist a scapegrace son who had dishonoured them.

I remembered hearing that on old Lord Braxted's death years ago, the Braxted estate was sold to the Merrion-Walters, who were ironfounders from Leeds.

No doubt the old man had cut his daughter off without the traditional shilling—but even so, some hundreds a year must have been theirs; what then did the poverty of of Alathea suggest? That some constant drain must be going on all the time.

Could Bobby Bulteel, the scapegrace, still be a gambler, and could that account for Alathea's poverty? This seemed the most probable explanation.

Then all over me there rushed a mad worship for my little love. Her splendid unselfishness, her noble self-sacrifice—her dignity, her serenity. I could have kissed the ground under her feet.

When Burton was undressing me I said to him—

"Did you ever know anything of the Hartelfords, Burton?—Bulteel is the family name."

"Can't say as I did personally, Sir Nicholas," he answered, "but of course when I was a young boy at Her Grace of Wiltshire's, before I came to your father, Sir Guy, I could not help hearing of the scandal about the cheating at cards.

"The whole nobility and gentry was put-to about it, and nothing else was talked of at dinner."

"Try to tell me what you remember of the story."

So Burton held forth in his own way for a quarter of an hour. There had been no possible doubt of the crime—it was the week after the Derby, and it was said that Bulteel had lost heavily.

He was caught red-handed and got off abroad that night, and the matter would probably have been hushed up but for the added sensation of Lady Hilda's elopement with him.

Mr. Marchant had been "all broken up" by it, and delayed the divorce so that, as far as Burton could remember, Captain Bulteel could not marry Lady Hilda for more than a year afterwards. All this coincided with what I already knew.

Lord Braxted died of a broken heart—it was said—leaving every cent to charity. The entail had been cut in the generation before and the title became extinct at his death.

I did not tell Burton then of my discovery, and lay long hours in the dark, thinking and thinking.

What did the Duchesse's attitude mean? In the eyes of the Duchesse de Courville-Hautevine, nee Adelaid de Mont Orgeuil—to cheat at cards would be the worst of all the cardinal sins. Such a man as Bobby Bulteel must be separated from his kind.

The Duchesse knew Lady Hilda probably (she often stayed in England with my mother), and she probably felt a disapproving pity for the poor lady.

The great charity of her mind would be touched by suffering, if the suffering was apparent, and perhaps she had some affection for the girl Alathea. But no affection could bridge the gulf which separated the child of an outcast from her world.

The sins of the father would inevitably be visited upon the children—by an unwritten law

—and although the Duchesse might love Alathea herself, she could not countenance her union with me.

The daughter of a man who had cheated at cards should go into a convent: Somehow, I instinctively felt that this would be her viewpoint.

Does Alathea know this tragedy about her father? Yes, of course, and she has to live always under this curse. Oh! the pity of it all.

Morning found me more restless and miserable than I have ever been before and it brought no sign of my love!

* * *

I passed some days in the cruellest unrest. There was no sign of Alathea. I allowed Maurice to drag me out into the world, and spent my evenings among my kind.

After an awful week, my old friend George Harcourt came back and dropped in to see me. I opened fire at once, and asked him to tell me all that he knew of the Bulteels, especially his old brother officer, Bobby.

"I have a particular reason for asking, George," I said.

"Very curious your speaking of them, Nicholas, because there has just been the devil of a fuss in the French Foreign Legion about that infernal blackguard; it came to my knowledge in my work."

"Has he been cheating at cards again?"

George nodded.

"Tell me from the beginning."

So he started—many of the bits I already knew. Lady Hilda had been a great friend of his and he dwelt upon the life of suffering she had had.

"There were a few years of frantic love and some sort of happiness, I expect, and then funds began to give out and Bobby's insane desire to gamble led them into the shadiest society.

"I happened upon them once or twice in my wanderings; then I lost sight of them for some years, and the next thing was someone told me the poor woman had broken down and was a nervous wreck.

"Two children had been born in quick succession, when the first one was about eleven years old—and the whole family were in miserable straits.

"Since then I have heard nothing, until the other day it came to my ears that the eldest girl —she must be over twenty now—is supporting the entire family. One of the children died lately —and now Bobby has put the cap on it. I am sorry for them, but Bobby is impossible."

"Oh! My poor little girl—what a life! How I long to take her out of it!

"When did you hear of this?"

"Only last night, and there will be a disgusting scandal, and the old story will be raked up."

"Can money keep it quiet, George?"

"I expect so, but who would be fool enough to pay for such a fellow?"

"I would, and will, if you can manage it without letting my name appear."

"My dear boy, how does it interest you? Why should you do such a quixotic thing? It is twenty-five thousand francs."

"Only twenty-five thousand francs! I'll give you the cheque this minute, George, if you can, in your own way, free the poor devil."

"But, Nicholas, you must be mad, my dear

boy! Or you have some strong motive I do not know of."

"Yes, I have. I want this chap freed from disaster, not for his sake but for the sake of the family. What must that poor lady have gone through, and that poor girl!"

George looked at me with his whimsical cynical eye.

"It's awfully decent of you, Nicholas," was all he said, though; and I reached for my chequebook and wrote a cheque for thirty thousand francs.

"You may need the extra five thousand, George, to make sure of the thing, and I count on you to patch it up as soon as you can."

He left after that, promising to see into the affair at once and telephone me the result, and when he had gone I tried to think over what it all meant.

Alathea did not know of this when I asked her to marry me last week. She must never know that I am paying, even if that makes matters easy enough for her to refuse me.

The reason for her long silence is that this fresh trouble has fallen upon them, I am sure. I felt so awfully, not being able to comfort her. The whole burden upon those young shoulders—

Just as I wrote that yesterday, Burton came in to say that Miss Sharp was in the little Salon and wished to see me—and I sent him to pray her to come in. I rose from my chair to bow to her when she entered—she never shakes hands. I was awfully pained to see the change in her.

Her poor little white face was thin and woebegone, and her lips were even paler, and her air was not so proud as usual.

"Won't you sit down," I said with whatever homage I could put into my voice.

She was so humbled and miserable that I knew she would even have taken off her glasses if I had asked her to, but of course I would not do that.

She seemed to find it hard to begin. I felt troubled for her, and so I started:

"I am awfully glad that you have come back."

She locked her hands together, in the shabby, black suede gloves.

"I have come to tell you that if you will give me twenty-five thousand francs this afternoon, I will accept your offer, and will marry you."

I held out my hand in my infinite joy, but I tried to control all other exhibition of emotion.

"That is awfully good of you. I can't say how I thank you," I said in a voice which sounded quite stern. "Of course I will give you anything in the world you want." Again I reached for my cheque-book, and wrote a cheque for fifty thousand and handed it to her.

She looked at it and went crimson.

"I do not want all that. Twenty-five thousand is enough. That is the price of the bargain."

I would not let this hurt me.

"Since you have consented to marry me, I have the right to give you what I please. You may need more than you have suggested, and I want everything to be smooth and as you would wish."

She trembled all over.

"I ... I cannot argue now. I must go at once ... but I will think over what I must say about it."

"If you are going to be my wife you must know that all that is mine will be yours, so how can a few thousand francs more or less now make any difference, though if you have any feeling concerning it, you can pay me back out of your first month's dress allowance!" and I tried to smile.

She started to her feet.

"When shall I see you again?" I pleaded.

"In two days."

"When will you marry me?"

"Whenever you arrange."

"Must you go now?"

"Yes—I must—I am grateful for your generosity. I will fulfil my side of the bargain."

"And I, mine."

I tried to rise, and she handed me my crutch, and then went towards the door, and there she turned.

"I will come on Friday at ten o'clock as usual. Good-bye," and she bowed and left me.

What a remarkable way to become an engaged man! But only joy filled me at that moment—I wanted to shout and sing—and to thank God!

Alathea will be mine, and surely it will only be a question of time before I can make her love me—my little girl!

I rang for Burton—I must have rung vigorously, for he came in hurriedly.

"Burton," I said, "congratulate me, my old friend. Miss Sharp has promised to marry me."

For once Burton's imperturbability deserted him—he almost staggered, and put his hand to his head.

"God bless my soul, Sir Nicholas," he gasped —and then went on—"Beg pardon, Sir, but that is the best piece of news I ever did hear in my life."

And his dear old eyes were full of tears—while he blew his nose vigorously.

"It will be a very quiet wedding, Burton."

"The wedding don't so much matter, Sir Nicholas—it is having the young lady always here to look after you."

"Without her glasses, Burton!"

"As you say, Sir—without them horn things." And there was a world of understanding in his old eyes.

He left the room presently with the walk of a boy, so elated was he—and I was left alone, thrilling in every nerve with triumph. How I long for Friday I cannot possibly say.

In the afternoon Maurice came to see me—and exclaimed at my improved appearance.

"Why, you look like a million dollars, Nicholas," Maurice said.

"I am getting well—that is all."

Maurice had an air of anxiety underneath his watchful friendliness.

"There is something, Nicholas—what? Was the clue of any use to you?"

"Yes, thank you a thousand times, Maurice. I could trace the whole thing. Miss Sharp comes of a very distinguished family, which I know all about. Her uncle is a miserable Earl—that is respectable enough—especially a tenth Earl! And her maternal grandfather was a Marquis."

"You were right then about the breeding. It always does show."

I had difficulty in not telling him my news, but I thought it wiser to remain silent until after Friday! Friday! Day of days!

Maurice suspected that there was something beyond in all this, and was not sure which course would be the best to pursue, one of sympathy or one of unconsciousness. He decided upon the latter and presently left me.

Then I telephoned to Cartier to have some rings sent up to look at. I have a feeling that I must be very discreet about giving Alathea presents, or she will be resentful, and even suspect that my bargain is not entirely a business one.

I suppose I had better not give her my mother's pearls until after the ceremony. I wonder if there will be a fuss when I suggest her going to the Rue de la Paix for clothes? I apprehend that there will be a stubborn resistance to almost everything I would wish to do.

How will the Duchesse take it? Probably philosophically, once it is an accomplished fact.

At that moment Burton brought me in a note from that very lady—I opened it eagerly, and its contents made me smile.

The Duchesse wrote to remind me of a promise I once made her: that if a certain family were in trouble, I would assist them to any amount—twenty-five thousand francs were now absolutely necessary on the moment; if I could send them to her by bearer, I would know that I was doing a good deed.

For the third time that day I reached for my cheque-book and wrote a cheque, but for only the sum asked on this occasion, and then when Burton had brought me note-paper, I sent a little word with it—to the Duchesse—and when I was alone again I laughed aloud.

I wonder how long it will take for my little love to come voluntarily into my arms?

Chapter
Eight

Saturday. I wonder how long I shall go on writing in this journal. I suppose once I should be happy it would not be necessary; well, the moment has not yet come, in spite of my being the fiancé of the woman I desire.

At ten o'clock I was waiting for her in the sitting-room, and I was thinking of that other time when I waited in anxiety, in case she did not return at all—this time I was very excited.

I heard Alathea's ring, and after she had taken off her hat she came into the room.

I believed that her anxieties must have been assuaged, because George Harcourt had telephoned late on Thursday night to say that he had been successful in paying off Bobby Bulteel's gambling debts, and that he had four thousand francs to hand back to me, the affair having been concluded for twenty-six thousand.

So what was my surprise to see Alathea's face below her glasses more woebegone than ever!

At first it gave me a stab of pain—does she really hate me so? She did not mention the money, so I wonder if it is that she does not yet know her father is cleared? I bowed as coldly as I used always to do, and she asked me if I had a chapter ready for her to type.

I answered that I had not, because I had been too busy with other things to have composed anything.

"I think we had better discuss the necessary arrangements for our marriage before we can settle down to our old work," I said.

"Very well."

"I shall have to have your full name and your father's and mother's and all that, you know, to make it legal. My lawyer will attend to all the formalities—they are quite considerable, I believe. He arrived from London on Monday. I got him a passport by pulling a lot of strings."

She actually trembled—it seemed as if the idea of all this had not come to her—some of the value of her sacrifice would be diminished if the family skeleton should be laid bare. I could see how she felt, so I reassured her.

"Believe me, I do not wish you to tell me anything about your family. As long as you can give just sufficient facts to satisfy the law, I have no curiosity to see your relations unless I can be of use."

"Thank you."

"I think a fortnight to three weeks is the quickest that everything can be settled in—will you marry me on the seventh of November, Miss Sharp?"

"Yes."

"Do you care for the church ceremony—or will the one at the Consulate do?"

"I should think that would be quite enough for us."

The ring cases were all lying upon the table by me; I pointed to them.

"I wonder if you would choose an engagement ring." I began opening the lids. "It is customary, you know," I went on as she started reluctantly; I intended to be firm with her in all the points where I had rights.

"Don't you think it is a little ridiculous?" she asked. "A ring for a mere business arrangement?"

I would not allow myself to be hurt, but I was conscious that I felt a little angry.

"You would prefer not to choose a ring, then? Very well, I will decide for you," and I took up one really magnificent single-stone diamond, set as only Cartier can set stones.

"This is the last thing in modernity," and I handed it to her. "A hard white diamond of egregious size, it cannot fail to be a reminder of our hard business bargain, and I shall ask you to be good enough to wear it."

"Am I to put it on now?"

"Please."

She did so, only she put it on her right third finger, her cheeks growing pink.

"Why do you do that?" I asked.

"What?"

"Put the ring on the wrong hand."

She changed it reluctantly, then she burst out:

"I suppose I ought to thank you for such a very splendid gift, but I can't because I would much rather not have it.

"Please do let us keep to business in every way, and please don't give me any more presents. I am going to be just your secretary with my wages commuted into some lump sum, I suppose."

I felt more angry—and I think she saw it. I remained silent, which forced her to speak.

"Do you intend that I shall live here, in the flat?"

"Of course. Will you please choose which of the two guest-rooms you would prefer. They both have bathrooms, and you will have the decoration redone as you wish."

Silence.

My exasperation augmented.

"Will you also please engage a maid and go and order every sort of clothes which you ought to have. I know, by the way you were dressed when I saw you in the Bois that Sunday, that your taste is perfect."

She stiffened as I spoke. It was quite plain to be seen that she loathed taking anything from me, but I had no intention of ceding a single point where I had the right to impose my will.

"You see, you will be known as my wife, therefore you must dress according to the position, and have everything my mother used to have. Otherwise, people would not respect you, and only think that you were invidiously placed."

Her cheeks flamed again at the last words.

"It is difficult to picture it all," she said. "Tell me exactly what you expect of me daily."

"I expect that when you have breakfasted, in your room if you wish, you will come and talk to me, perhaps do a little writing or go out to drive, or what you wish, and that we shall lunch, and in the afternoon do whatever turns up.

"You will want to go out and see your friends and do what you please. And perhaps you will play to me as often as you feel inclined, and after dinner we can go to the theatre, or read, or do whatever you like.

"As soon as my treatments with these doctors are concluded, and I have my new leg and eye, and we shall hope war is finished, we can travel, or go back to England. Then I shall begin taking up a political career.

"And I shall hope you will take a real interest in that and help me as though I were your brother."

"Very well."

"You will order the clothes today?"

"Yes."

She was subdued now. The programme was not very formidable, except in that it contained daily companionship with me.

"Have you told the Duchesse de Courville-Hautevine yet that we are engaged?" I asked after a moment's pause.

Discomfort grew in her manner.

"No."

"Do you think that she will not approve of the marriage?"

"She may not."

"Perhaps you would rather that I told her?"

"As you please."

"I want you to understand something quite clearly—Alathea"—she started when I said her name—"and that is that I expect you to treat me with confidence, and tell me anything which you think that I ought to know, so that we neither of us can be put in a false position.

"Beyond that, believe me, I have no curiosity—I desire a companionship of brain, and a sort of permanent secretary who does not feel hostile all the time, that is all."

I could see that she was controlling herself with all her will, and that she was overwrought and intensely troubled. I knew that some barrier

was between us which I could not at present sur-
mount. All she said after a minute was—

"How did you know my name was Alathea?"

"I heard your little sister call you that the
day I saw you in the Bois; I think it a very beautiful name."

Silence.

Her discomfort seemed to come to a climax,
for after a little she spoke.

"The twenty-five thousand francs beyond
the twenty-five I asked you for—I cannot return
to you—I feel very much about it, and that you
should pay for my clothes, and give me presents.
It is the hardest thing I have ever had to do in my
life—to take all this."

"Do not let it bother you, I am quite content with the bargain. Perhaps you would rather
go now after we have selected which room you
will have."

"Thank you."

She gave me my crutch, and I led the way
and she followed. I knew instinctively that she
would choose the room which was furthest from
mine. She did!

"This will do," she said immediately we entered it.

"The look-out is not so nice, it only gets the
early morning sun," I ventured to remark.

"It is quieter."

"Very well."

"It was rather arranged for a man and is perhaps severe. Do you wish anything changed?"

She did not appear to take any more interest
in it than if it had been a hotel room.

"I don't want anything altered—thank you."

When we got back to the sitting-room, I offered to send the carriage for her to go and do her shopping, but she refused, and I thought it was wiser to let her go.

Presently we shall have years in which to talk, and there is always the danger of our coming to an open rupture, and the bargain being off —if we see too much of each other now.

"Good-bye," she said a little nervously, and I bowed and said, "Good-bye," and she went from the room.

And when she had gone I laughed aloud, and began to analyse the situation.

George Harcourt has paid the gambling debt, therefore the fifty thousand I gave Alathea cannot have been used for that—some fresh worry is perhaps upon the wretched family.

The obvious thing for me to do is to go and see the Duchesse—and yet I have some strange sort of wish that it should be Alathea herself who tells me everything, and not that she becomes aware, by inference, that I must know.

I feel that our future happiness depends upon her giving up all this stubborn pride. What is at the back of her mind?

I am sure she thinks that Suzette is my mistress still, and this insults her, but she reasons that with the bargain as it is, she has not the smallest right to object. She is furious with herself to think that it should matter to her.

That is a thought! Why indeed should it matter if she is utterly indifferent to me? Is it possible? Can it be that— No, I dare not think of it, but, in any case, it will be the most thrilling situation, once she is my wife.

I believe it would be wisest for me not to go to the Duchesse's, but simply write to her a note telling her of my news, and then anything she may tell me will be gratuitous.

I had just finished doing this when once again a letter was brought in from that lady, and this time it was to thank me for my cheque and to tell me that it had been the means of preventing a most disagreeable scandal, and bringing peace to the family!

Sardonic mirth overcame me. So three separate people seemed to be under the impression that they had paid this gambler's debts! Each apparently unaware that there was anyone else in the running!

It looks as if "Bobby" has wolfed the lot! Does Alathea know, and is this the extra cause of her worry?

I sent my note back by the Duchesse's messenger, who still waited—and then I went to my luncheon.

In about an hour the telephone rang—a request from the Hotel de Courville that I should repair there immediately without fail.

"Her Grace spoke herself," Burton said, "and said it was most important, Sir Nicholas."

"Very well, order the carriage. By the way, Burton, did you congratulate Miss Sharp?"

Burton coughed.

"I did make so bold, Sir Nicholas, as to tell the young lady how very glad I was, but she took it queer-like—she stiffened up and said it was only a business arrangement, to be able to write your letters and do your work without people talking about it. That seemed funny to me, so I said nothing more."

"Burton, it is funny for the moment—Miss Sharp is only marrying me for some reason for her family—the same one which forces her to work—but I hope I can make her think differently about it someday."

"Pardon the liberty I am taking, Sir Nicholas —but perhaps she don't like the idea of Mamzelle —and don't know she's gone for good."

"That is probably the case."

Burton's wise old face expressed complete understanding as he left the room, and presently I was on my way to the Hotel de Courville—a sense of exhilaration, excitement, and joy in my heart!

* * *

The Duchesse was playing impatiently with her glasses when I was announced by the servant of ninety! Her face expressed some strong feeling. I was not sure if it was tinged with displeasure or no.

"Nicholas—explain yourself. You tell me you are engaged to your secretary! So this has been going on all the time, and you have not told me —I, who was your mother's oldest friend!"

"Dear Duchesse—you are mistaken—it has only just been settled. No one was more surprised at my offer than Miss Sharp herself."

"You know her real name, Nicholas? And her family history? You have guessed, of course, from my asking you for the twenty-five thousand francs, that they were in some difficulty?"

"Yes—I know Alathea is the daughter of the Honourable Robert and Lady Hilda Bulteel."

"She has told you all the story perhaps, but you cannot know what the money was for, because the poor child does not know it herself. It is more just that I should inform you, since you are going to marry into the family."

"Thank you, Duchesse."

She then began, and gave me a picture of her old friendship with Lady Hilda, and of the dreadful calamity which had befallen in her going off with Bobby Bulteel.

"It was one of those cases of mad love, Nicholas—which fortunately seem to have died out of the modern world.

"One could not, of course, acknowledge them for a crime like that—but I have ever been so fond of poor Hilda and that sweet little child.

"She was born here in this hotel, poor Hilda came to me in her great trouble, and I was in deep mourning myself then for my husband, and the house is large, and it could all pass quietly."

I reached forward and took the Duchesse's hand and kissed it, and she went on:

"Alathea is my godchild, one of my names is Alathea; the poor little one, she adored her father in all those first years.

"She was about twelve when she heard of her father's crime. She was the gayest, most sweet child before that, through all their poverty—but from that moment her character changed.

"It destroyed something in her spirit which one must believe. She set firmly to education, decided she would be a secretary, cultivated herself, and worked and worked. She worshipped her mother and resented immensely her father's treatment of her."

"She must always have had a wonderful character."

"For that—yes." The Duchesse paused a moment, then went on:

"Quite a tremendous character, and as Bobby sank and poor Hilda became more ill, and wretched, that child rose in strength, and supported them all—since the war came, they have almost lived upon her earnings—the father is without conscience—and of a selfishness unspeakable.

"And now that brute has again cheated at cards—and poor Hilda came to me in her great distress—and remembering your words, Nicholas —I called upon you. Hilda took the money and gave it to this infamous husband, and the affair was settled that night. Alathea knows nothing about it."

Light was dawning upon me. The admirable Bobby had evidently played upon the feelings of both wife and daughter!

"Duchesse, why did you not wish me to know the real name, and would not help me at all about 'Miss Sharp'—won't you now tell me your reason?"

The Duchesse shaded her eyes from the fire with a hand-screen, and it came between us, and I could not see her face, but her voice changed.

"I was greatly surprised to find the girl in your flat one day—I had not understood with whom she was working; I was not pleased about it—frankly, Nicholas, one cannot help knowing of your existence and your friends.

"And I feared your interest for a secretary— might be—as for—them—and I disliked that my godchild should run such a risk."

Suddenly I saw myself and the utterly rotten life I had led. I could not even be indignant with the Duchesse, judging me from that standpoint.

She was right, but I did tell her that men had a slightly different angle in looking upon such things in England, where women worked, and were respected, and the idea of making love to any secretary would never have entered my head.

"You are pleased now, though, dear Duchesse!" I pleaded.

"I would not have encouraged it, but since it is done, I can but wish my dear Alathea and you, my dear boy, true happiness."

Again I took and kissed her kind hand.

"In England, especially in this war time, questions are not asked, *n'est-ce pas?* She can be 'Sharp' simply and not 'Bulteel'—then it may pass.

"For the girl herself, you have a rare jewel, Nicholas, unselfish, devoted, true, but with the will of the devil! You shall not be able to turn her as you wish, if her ideas go the other way!"

"Duchesse, the situation is peculiar. There is no question of love in it. Alathea is marrying me merely so that she may give money to her family. I am marrying so that I may have a secretary without scandal. We are not going to be really husband and wife."

The Duchesse dropped her fire-screen. Her clever eyes were whimsical and sparkling.

"*Tiens!*" she said, and never has the delicious word conveyed so much meaning! "You believe that truly, Nicholas? Alathea is a very pretty girl."

"I asked her to marry me under those terms, and it was only upon those terms she accepted me."

The Duchesse laughed.

"A nice romance! Well, my son, I wish you joy!"

"Duchesse—" and I leaned forward, "do you really think I can make her love me? Am I too awful? Is there a chance?"

The Duchesse patted my arm and her face shone with kindliness.

"Of course, foolish boy!"

When I left the Hotel de Courville it had been arranged that the Duchesse would receive my wife with honour—her world knowing only that I had married an English "Miss Sharp."

I heard no more of my fianceé until next morning, when she telephoned. Did I wish her to come that day?

Burton answered that I hoped she would, about eleven o'clock.

I intended to tell her that I thought it might be wiser now if she did not come again until the wedding, as once we were engaged I would not allow her to run the risk of meeting anyone and giving a false impression—I think the strain would be too great in any case.

I did not come into the Salon until she was there, and she rose as I entered. She was whiter than ever, and very stern.

"I have been thinking," she said, before I could speak—"that if I promise to fulfill the bargain, and—live here in the flat—with you—going through the ceremony at the Consulate is quite unnecessary.

"Your caprice of having me for your wife merely in name in England may pass, and it seems ridiculous to be tied—I am quite indifferent to what anyone thinks of me—I would prefer it like that."

"Why?" I asked, and wondered for a moment what had occurred.

"There are so many stupid law things, if there is a marriage—and if you have the same from me without, surely you see that that is better."

I first thought that it was this fear of my knowing her family history which was at the root of this suggestion, but then I remembered that she would know that I would hear it in any case from the Duchesse. What then could it be?

I felt cruel—I was not going to make things too easy for her. If she had the will of the devil, she had also the pride!

"If you are indifferent to such an invidious position as your new idea would place us in, I am not—I do not wish my friends to think that I am such a cad as presumably to have taken advantage of your being my secretary."

"You wish to go on with the marriage then?"

"Of course."

She clasped her hands together suddenly, as if she could control herself no longer—and I thought of what she had said to Burton about feeling that she could not fight any more. I would not allow myself to sympathise with her.

I was longing in every nerve of my being to take her into my arms and tell her that I loved her and that I knew everything, but I would not do this.

I cannot let her master me, or we shall never have any peace—I will not tell her that I love her until her pride is broken and I have made her love me and come to me voluntarily.

She was silent.

"I have informed the Duchesse de Courville-Hautevine that we are engaged—I saw her yesterday."

She started perceptibly.

"She has told you my real name?"

"I have known that for some time. I thought I had made it plain to you that I am not interested about the subject—we need not mention it again.

"You have only to talk to old Robert Nelson, my lawyer, when he comes on Monday—he will tell you the settlements I propose to make, and you can discuss with him as to whether or not you think them satisfactory.

"Perhaps you on your side will tell me what reason you have that is strong enough to make a girl of your natural self-respect be willing to take the position of my apparent—mistress?"

She burst out for a second, throwing out her hands, then controlled herself.

"No, I won't tell you—I will tell you nothing —I will just stick to the bargain if I must. You have no right to my thoughts, only my actions!"

I bowed—disagreeable as she was, there was a distinctly pleasant zest in fighting!

"Perhaps of your courtesy, you will take off those glasses now, since I am aware that you only wear them to conceal your eyes, and not that they are necessary for your sight—"

She flushed with annoyance.

"And if I refuse?"

I shrugged my shoulders.

"I shall think it very childish of you."

With a petulance which I had never seen in her, she tossed her head.

"I don't care—at present I will not."

I frowned, but did not speak. This will be discussed between us later—my fighting spirit is up—she *shall* obey me!

"Did you order the clothes yesterday?"

"Yes."

"Enough, I hope."

"Yes."

"Well, now, I have a suggestion to make which I am sure will please you, and that is that you will appoint some meeting-place with Mr Nelson for Tuesday morning.

"Since you do not trust my good taste far enough to let me know your home address—perhaps at the Hotel de Courville, if the Duchesse will permit—and after that, then we do not meet again until the seventh of November at the ceremony.

"Mr Nelson will arrange with you all the necessities of the law, and what witnesses you must have. This will save these useless discussions and give you a little breathing space."

This seemed to subdue her and she agreed less defiantly.

"And now I will not detain you longer," I said stiffly. "*Au revoir* until the seventh of November, at whatever hour is arranged, or if we must meet before at the signing of the contract," and I bowed.

She bowed also, and walked haughtily to the door, and left.

And greatly exhilarated, I decided to go and lunch with Maurice at the Ritz.

I did not tell Maurice of my approaching wedding. I have a plan that he shall know only when I ask him to come to the Hotel de Courville to be presented to my wife.

As I drove back to my flat, taking a roundabout way through the Bois, I mused about many things.

What will Alathea do I wonder during the fortnight of our engagement? I feel that I can afford to wait with patience and certainty.

But the thought that I do not even know my fiancée's address—and that she is resentful and defiant, and rebellious at everything, and yet intends to marry me, on the seventh of November—it is really almost humorous!

And now it behoves me to put my house in order and map out exactly what I mean to do!

Chapter
Nine

The days go slowly on—my preparations are complete. My good friend Nelson arrived on Monday and took charge of the affair. He was entirely *au courant* with the Bulteel story—it was the great scandal of twenty-five years ago.

He expressed no opinion as to my marrying into such a family, but went about the business end with diligence.

I made a very nice settlement upon Alathea, more than he thought was necessary. Then he spoke of arrangements for possible children and fixed that too. I wonder what she will say when she reads that part!

Now I am beginning to wonder what Alathea would prefer to do. I don't want to see her until the ceremony, but I suppose I must.

* * *

The Duchesse has arranged that I should meet my fiancée in her sitting-room and sign the contract there on the day before the wedding—five days from now. Alathea, she tells me, is like a frozen image—but faithful to her promise to me.

My dear old friend has not made any comment or tried to aid matters. I think she rejoices that I shall have such an interesting time in the breaking down of the barrier.

I feel quite serene—Alathea will be mine—she cannot get away from me. I can insidiously, from day to day, carry out my plan of winning her—and the tougher the fight is, the more it will be worthwhile afterwards!

November 6

Today was really wonderful! Mr Nelson has presumably seen Alathea and her family several times—I have refused to hear anything about it—and he arrived with her alone at the Hotel de Courville.

The Duchesse and I were talking when the two were announced. Alathea was in a nice little grey frock and had her glasses on—I think she knew the Duchesse would not approve of that camouflage, because there was an air of defiance about her.

Her rebellious Cupid's bow of a mouth was shut sternly—she was even quite repellent—she had never attracted me more!

The Duchesse was sweet to her and made no remark about the glasses, but was called back to the ward almost immediately for a little—and while she was gone, Mr Nelson read over the settlement.

"I think you are giving me a great deal too much," Alathea said annoyedly. "I shall feel uncomfortable—and chained."

"I intend my wife to have this," I answered quietly. "So I am afraid you will have to agree."

She pulled in her lips, but said no more until the part about the children came, when she started to her feet—her cheeks crimson and her eyes flashing.

"What is this ridiculous clause?" she asked angrily.

Old Mr Nelson looked unspeakably shocked. "It is customary in all marriage settlements, my dear young lady," he said reprovingly.

Alathea looked at me with suspicion but she said nothing; and the Duchesse returning then to the room, all was soon signed, sealed, and delivered—and Mr Nelson withdrew, saying he would call for Miss Bulteel next day for the wedding.

When we were alone the Duchesse kissed us both.

"I hope for your happiness, my children," she said. "I know you both, and your droll characters —the time will come when you may know each other, and in any case I feel that you will both remember that a realisation of correct behaviour helps all situations in life. And the rest is in the hands of the *bon Dieu*."

Then she left us again. Alathea sat stiffly down upon an uncompromising little Louis XV *canapé* out of my reach. I did not move or speak; indeed, I lit a cigarette casually.

Alathea's face was a study, and I watched her lazily. How had I ever thought her plain?— even in those first days, disguised with the horn spectacles and the torn-back hair—the contour of her little face is so perfectly oval, and her neck so round and long, but not too long.

There is not the least look of scragginess about her, just extreme slenderness, a small-boned creature of perhaps five feet four or five, with childish outline.

Today in the becoming little grey frock, and even with the glasses on, she is lovely—perhaps she seems so to me because I now know that the glasses are not necessary.

The expression of her mouth said, "Am I being tricked? Does the man mean to seize me when he gets me alone? Shall I run away and have done with it?"

She was restless—her old serenity seemed to have deserted her.

"I wanted to ask you," I began calmly, "what you would like to do immediately after the wedding—I mean would you prefer that we went to Versailles—the passport business makes everything so difficult—or would you rather go down to the Riviera? Or just stay at the flat?"

"I don't care in the least," she replied ungraciously.

"Then if you don't care we will stay at the flat, because if I do not interrupt my treatment I shall be the sooner well to go to England. Have you engaged a maid?"

"Yes . . ."

"You will give orders that your trunks are sent in in the morning, then, and that she has everything ready for you."

"Very well."

All this time her face was turned away from me as much as possible. For one second a fear came to me that after all perhaps it is real hate she has for me, which will be insurmountable, and I was impelled to ask her—

"Alathea—do you detest the idea of marrying me so much that you would rather break the whole thing?"

She turned and faced me now, blue fire com-

ing from those beautiful eyes, I am sure, could
I have seen them!

"It is not a question of what I would wish
or not—nor of my feelings in any way. I am going
through with the ceremony, and shall be your
permanent secretary, because I am under great
monetary obligations to you, and wish for security for my family in the future.

"You put it to me that you wanted to buy
me and I could name the price—you have over-
paid it. I shall not go back upon my promise—
only I want to feel perfectly sure that you will expect nothing more of me than what we have arranged."

"I shall expect nothing more," I replied, "your
sense of the fitness of things will suggest to you
not to make either of us look ridiculous in public by
your being over-disagreeable to me—we shall carry on with a semblance of mutual respect, I
hope."

She bowed.

The temptation to burst out and tell her of
my feelings was extraordinary—I absolutely trembled with the control it required not to rise from
my chair and go and take her hands; but I re-
strained every sign and appeared as indifferent
as she.

The Duchesse came back in a few moments
and I said I would go.

And now I am alone before the crackling fire
in my sitting-room—and I wonder how many men
have spent the eve of their marriage in so quiet a
manner.

At that moment the telephone rang, and
George Harcourt asked if he might come round
and smoke a cigar.

When we were settled in two comfortable armchairs before the fire, he held forth as usual. He had arranged the affairs of Bobby Bulteel only in the nick of time. "I have all the receipts, Nicholas, to hand to you," he said.

"The wretched creature was overcome with gratitude. We had a long chat—and he plans to clear out and start life afresh in the Argentine as soon as war is over and he can resign his commission.

"He agreed to leave the family here unmolested now and not to return to them for years."

Then I told my old friend that I intended to marry the daughter on the morrow—he was very surprised.

"I could not imagine what your interest could be, Nicholas, unless it had something to do with a woman—but where did you ever meet the girl, my dear boy?"

I explained.

"You might come to the wedding, George," I said.

He promised he would.

Then our talk drifted to politics and the war, and it was just about midnight before old George left, and when he had gone I opened the window wide, and looked out on the night.

There was a half-moon almost set—and the air was still, and very warm for the beginning of November.

I found myself saying a prayer that I might be true to my trust, and have strength enough of will to wait patiently until my Alathea comes voluntarily into my arms.

And how I wonder what she is thinking about —there—at Auteuil?

I went along into the room which is to be hers

tomorrow, and I saw that it was all arranged, except the flowers, which would come in fresh in the morning. And then I hobbled back to my own room and rang for Burton—the faithful creature waits for me no matter how late I am.

When I was safely in bed, he came over to me, and his dear old face showed emotion.

"I do indeed wish you happiness, Sir Nicholas, tomorrow will be the best day of my life."

We shook hands silently—and he left me, still writing in this journal.

I feel no excitement, but rather as if another act in the drama of life has ended, that is all, and that tomorrow I am starting upon a new one which will decide whether the end of the play shall be tragedy or—content.

* * *

I am not going to describe the wedding in this journal—a civil ceremony is not interesting in its baldness. I had literally no emotions, and Alathea looked as pale as her white cloth frock.

She wore a little sable toque and a big sable cloak I had sent her the night before, by Nelson— the ring was the new diamond hoop set in platinum—no more gold fetters for modern girls!

George Harcourt and Mr Nelson were our witnesses—and the whole thing was over in a few minutes—and we were being congratulated.

Burton's was by far the happiest face there, as he helped me into the automobile—lent by the Embassy; Alathea had just shaken hands with Mr Nelson and been wished joy by George.

"May you know every happiness, Lady Thormonde," he said. "Take care of Nicholas and make him quite well, he is the best fellow on earth."

Alathea thanked him coldly. He is such a citizen of the world that he showed no surprise —and finally we were off on our way to the flat.

Burton had been beside the chauffeur to help me in and out, and while we had been driving Alathea had not spoken a word. She had turned from me, and her little body was drawn back as far in the corner as possible.

My own emotions were queer—I did not feel actually excited. I felt just as I used to when we were taking up a new position in a very ticklish part of the Line.

The maid Alathea had engaged arrived in the morning, and I had had the loveliest flowers put in all the rooms—Pierre intended to outdo himself for the wedding *déjeuner*, I knew—and Burton had been able to find from somewhere a really respectable-looking footman, not too obviously wounded!

Alathea handed me my crutch as we got out of the lift. Perhaps she thinks this is going to be one of her new duties!

We went straight into the sitting-room, and I sat down in my chair.

Her maid, named Henriette, had taken her cloak and hat in the hall, and I suppose from sheer nervousness, and to cover the first awkward moments, Alathea buried her face in the big bowl of roses on a table near another armchair before she sat down in it.

"What lovely flowers!" she said. They were the first words she had spoken to me directly.

"I wondered what would be your favourites. You must tell me for the future. I just had roses because they happen to be mine."

"I like roses best too."

I was silent for quite two minutes. She tried

to keep still, then I spoke and I could hear a tone of authority in my voice.

"Alathea, again I ask you please to remove your glasses, as I told you before I know that you wear them only so that I may not see your eyes, not for sight or light or anything.

"To keep them on is a little undignified and ridiculous now, and irritates me very much."

She coloured and straightened herself.

"To remove my glasses was not part of the bargain—you should have made it a condition if you had wanted to impose it. I do not admit that you have the least right to ask me to take them off, and I prefer to wear them."

"For what possible reason?"

"I will not tell you."

I felt my temper rising. If I had not been a cripple I could not have resisted the temptation to rise and seize her in my arms, tear the d——d things off! and punish her with a thousand kisses.

As it was I felt an inward rage—what a fool I had been not to have actually made the removal of them a sine qua non before I signed the contract!

"It is very ungenerous of you, and shows a spirit of hostility which I think we agreed that you would drop."

Silence.

The desire to punish her physically—beat her, to make her obey me—was the only thing I felt. A nice emotion for a wedding day!

"Do you mean to wear them all the time— even when we go out in the world?" I asked when I could control my voice.

"Probably."

"Very well, then. I consider you are breaking the bargain in the spirit, if not in the letter. You yourself said you were going to be my permanent secretary—no secretary in the world would insist upon doing something she knew to be a great irritation to her employer."

Silence.

"You are only lowering yourself in my estimation by showing this obstinacy. Since we have now to live together, I would rather not have to grow to despise you for childishness."

She started to her feet, and with violence threw the glasses onto the table. Her beautiful eyes flashed at me—the lashes are that peculiar curly kind, not black, but soft and dusky, a little lighter near the skin.

The eyes themselves are intensely blue, and with everything of passion and magnetism and attraction in them. It is no wonder she wore glasses while having to face the world by herself.

A woman with eyes like that would not be safe alone in any avocation where men could observe her. I have never seen such expressive, fascinating eyes in my life. I thrilled in every fibre of my being, and with triumph also to think that our first battle should be won!

"Thank you," I said, making my voice very calm. "I had grown so to respect your balance and serenity that I should have been sorry to have to change my opinion."

I could see that she was palpitating with fury at having been made to obey. I felt it wise to turn the conversation.

"I suppose lunch will be ready soon."

She went towards the door then, and left me —I wondered what she would say when she got to her room and found the three sapphire bangles waiting for her on the dressing-table!

I had written on a card inside the lid of the box—

"To Alathea, with her husband's best wishes."

Burton announced lunch before she returned to the sitting-room. I sent him to say that it was ready—and a moment later she came in. She had the case in her hand, which she put down on the table; and her cheeks were very pink, her eyes she kept lowered.

"I wish you would not give me presents," she gasped a little breathlessly, coming close up to my chair. "I do not care to receive them, you have loaded me with things, the sables, the diamond ring, the clothes—everything—and now these."

I took the case and opened it, removing the bangles.

"Give me your wrist," I said sternly.

She looked at me, too much surprised at my tone to speak.

I put out my hand and took her bare arm—her sleeves were to the elbows—and I deliberately put the three bracelets on while she stood petrified.

"I have had enough of your disagreeable temper," I said in the same voice. "You will wear these, and anything else I choose to give you, though your rudeness will soon remove my desire to give you anything."

She was absolutely flabbergasted, but I had touched her pride.

"I apologise if I have seemed rude," she said at last. "I—suppose you have the right, really—only—"

Her whole slender body quivered with a wave of rebellion.

"Let us say no more about the matter, but go

in to lunch—only you will find that I am not such a weakling as you no doubt supposed you would have to deal with."

I hobbled up from my chair—Burton discreetly not having entered the room. Alathea gave me my crutch—and we went into the dining-room.

While the servants were there I led the conversation upon the war news, an ordinary subject —and she played the game; but when we were alone with the coffee, I filled her glass with Benedictine, which she had refused when Burton handed the liqueurs. She had taken no wine at all.

"Now drink whatever toast you like," I told her. "I am going to drink one to the time when you don't hate me so much, and we can have a little quiet friendship and peace."

She sipped her glass, and her eyes became inscrutable. What she was thinking of I do not know.

I find myself watching those eyes all the time. Every reflection passes through them, they are as expressive of all shades of emotion as are the eyes of a cat—though the beautiful Madonna tenderness I have never seen again since the day when she held the child in her arms, and I was rude to her.

When we went back to the Salon I knew that I was passionately in love with her. Her restiveness is absolutely alluring, and excites all my hunting instinct. She looks quite lovely, and the subtle magnetism which drew me the first days, even when she appeared poor and shabby, and red of hand, is stronger than ever.

I felt that I wanted to crush her in my arms and devour her—the blood thumped in my temples—I had to use every atom of my will with myself, and lay back in my chair and closed my eye.

She went straight to the piano and began to play. It seemed as though she were talking, telling me of the passion in her soul.

She played weird Russian pieces and crashed agonising chords—then she played laments, and finally a soft and soothing thing of McDowall's, and every note had found an echo in me—and I had followed, it almost seemed, all her pain.

"You play divinely, child," I said, when she had finished. "I am going to rest now—will you give me some tea later on?"

"Yes," and her voice was quite meek—while she helped me with my crutch, and I went to the door of my room.

"I would like you to wear nice soft tea-gowns. My eye gets so wearied with everything bright after a while. I hope you have got all you want and that your room is comfortable."

"Yes, thank you."

I bowed and went on into my room and shut the door. Burton was waiting to help me to lie down.

"It has been a very tiring day for you, Sir Nicholas," he said, "and for Her Ladyship also."

"Go and have a rest yourself, Burton—you have been up since cock-crow—the new man, Antoine, can call me at five." And soon I was in a land of blissful dreams.

Of course it was the very irony of fate that Suzette should have selected this very afternoon to come in and thank me for the villa she had bought with the cheque I had given her.

Antoine opened the door to her while Burton

was out. I heard afterwards that she told him she had an appointment with me when he had hesitated about letting her in.

Antoine came to my room by the passage, and said a lady was in the Salon to see me by appointment.

It was just growing dim in the Salon, about half past four o'clock, and a figure rose from the sofa by the fire as I entered.

"*Mon chou!—mon petit chéri!*" I heard simultaneously with a softly closing sound of the door behind the screen which masks the entrance to the room from the hall; Antoine leaving, I supposed then—probably Alathea, I surmised afterwards!

"Suzette!" I exclaimed angrily. "Why do you come here?"

She flew to me and held out her arms—expressing affection and grateful thanks. She had come for no other reason but to express her friendly appreciation!

To get rid of her was all I desired! I never was more angry, but to show it would have been the poorest game. I did not tell her it was my wedding day, I just said I was expecting some relatives, and that I knew she would understand and would go at once.

"Of course," she said, and shook me by the hand.

"It must be the very last time, Suzette," I said. "I have given you all that you wanted and I would rather not see you again."

She pouted—but agreed.

I prayed that Alathea had been unaware of my visitor.

I waited until five, and then went back into the sitting-room to my chair, and Antoine brought in the tea, and turned on the lights, and a moment or two afterwards Alathea came in.

Her eyes were stony, and as she advanced up the room she sniffed the air disgustedly, her fine nostrils quivering. Suzette's pungent perfume was no doubt still present to one coming from outside.

Hauteur, contempt, and disgust expressed themselves in my little darling's blue eyes.

She wore a soft lavender frock, and was utterly delectable; and when I reflected that but for this impassable barrier which my own action in the past had been the means of erecting between us, I might now have made her love me.

And that on this, our wedding day, she might have been coming into my arms—I could have groaned aloud.

"May I open the window?" she said with the air of an offended Empress.

"Yes—do—open it wide," and then I laughed aloud cynically. I could as easily have cried.

Alathea would not, of course, have spoken about her impression—to do so would have inferred that she took an interest in me beyond that of a secretary—every impression she always has given me is that nothing in my life can matter to her one jot.

But I know that this affair of Suzette does matter to her.

She resents it because she is a woman—and how I wish I might believe that it is because she is not as indifferent towards me as she pretends.

She poured out the tea. I expect my face looked like the devil—I did not speak—I knew I was frowning angrily. A rising wind blew the curtain out and banged the window.

She got up and shut it, then she threw some

cedar dust on the fire from the box in which it is kept on a table near. She has seen Burton do this, no doubt. I love the smell of cedar burning.

The room looked so comfortable and home-like—with its panelling of old pitch-pine, cleaned of its paint and mellowed and waxed so that it looks like deep amber showing up the greyish pear-wood carvings, one might have been in some room of old England of about 1699.

Everything looked the setting for a love scene. The glowing lamps, apricot-shaded, and the firelight, and the yellow roses everywhere—and two human beings who belonged to each other and were young, and not cold of nature.

Sitting there with faces of stone; and in each one's heart, bitterness. Again I laughed aloud.

The mocking sound seemed to disturb my bride—she allowed her tea-cup to rattle as she put it down nervously.

The silence became oppressive, so I asked, "Will it interest you going to England?"

"I dare say."

"I have a place there, you know—shall you care to live in it after war is over."

"I believe it is the duty of people to live in their homes if they have inherited them as a trust."

"I believe I can always count upon you to do your duty."

"I hope so."

Then I exerted myself and talked to her about politics and what were my views and aims—she entered into this stiffly, and so an hour passed. But all the time I could feel that her inner self was disturbed, and more resentful and rebellious than ever.

We had been two puppets making conversation all the time—neither had said anything naturally.

At last the pretence ended and we went to our separate rooms to dress for dinner.

Burton had returned by now—and I told him of the detestable thing which had happened—at which he was much concerned.

"Best of her sort was Mamzelle, Sir Nicholas; but I've always said they bring trouble, every one of them—if I may make so bold!"

And as I hobbled back into the Salon to meet my wife for our first dinner alone, once more I heartily agreed with him!

* * *

Alathea looked perfectly lovely when she came into the Salon dressed for dinner. She had a gauzy tea-gown on, of a shade of blue like her eyes. Her nut-brown hair was beautifully done, showing her tiny head.

Whether she likes it or no, I must give her some pearl ear-rings—and my mother's pearls—that will be a moment! But I had better wait a little while.

Her eyes were shining with excitement or resentment, or a mixture of both. She was purely feminine. She intended to attract me, I am certain —her subconscious mind did, at all events, even though she would not have admitted it to herself. She was smarting still about Suzette.

The situation fills her with distrust and uneasiness; but I know now, after analysing every point when I could not sleep last night, that she is not really indifferent to me. And it is because she is not, that she is angry.

I registered a vow that I would *make* her love me without explaining about Suzette—fate can let her find out for herself.

I had troubled to put on a tail-coat and white waistcoat, not a dinner jacket as usual—and had even a buttonhole of a gardenia—found by Burton for this great occasion!

I looked into her eyes with my one blue one, which is, I suppose, as blue as her own. She instantly averted her glance.

"I cannot offer you my arm, Milady," I said rather sarcastically. "So we will have to go in one after the other."

She bowed and led the way.

The table was too beautifully decorated, and the dinner a masterpiece!—while the champagne was iced to perfection, and the burgundy was a poem! The pupils of Alathea's eyes, before the partridge came, were black as night.

Burton discreetly marshalled Antoine out of the room each time after the dishes were handed.

"When will you get your new eye?" my wife —I like to write that!—asked in the first interval when we were alone—"and your new leg?"

"In a day or two. It will be so wonderful to walk again."

"I should think so—"

Then something seemed to strike her suddenly, of how hateful it must all have been for me. Her hard expression changed and she almost whispered—

"It—will seem like a new life."

"I mean to make a new life—if you will help me, I want to get away from all the old useless days. I want to do things which are worthwhile."

"Shall you soon go into Parliament?"

"I suppose it will take a year or two, but we

shall begin to pave the way directly we go back to England—and I hope that will be for Christmas."

She avoided looking at me—I could never catch her eye, but her adorable little profile was good enough to contemplate—the crisp curl by her ear delighted me, and another in the nape of her neck filled me with wild longings to kiss it and the pearly skin beneath it!

I think I deserve great praise for the way I acted, for the whole thing was acting. I was as cold and haughty and aloof as she was herself; but I used every art I knew of to draw her out and make her talk.

She is such a lady that she fell into the stride and spoke politely, as if to some stranger who had taken her in to dinner at a party.

At last we talked of the Duchesse—and we discussed her interesting character—such a survival of the Ancien Régime!

"She is so very good and charitable," Alathea said, "and has always a twinkle in her eye which carries her through things."

"You laugh sometimes, too?" I asked with assumed surprise. "That is delightful. I adore the 'twinkle in the eye,' but I was afraid you would never unbend far enough so that we could laugh together!"

I think this offended her.

"Life would be impossible without a sense of humour—even if it is a grim one."

"Well, nothing need be grim any more—and we can both smile at the rather absurd situation between us—which, however, suits us both admirably. You will never interfere with me, nor I with you."

"No ..." There was a tone in this which let

me feel that her thoughts had harked back to Suzette.

"The Duchesse is going to have a little tea-party for us on Saturday you know, so that you may be introduced as my wife."

Alathea became embarrassed at once.

"Will people know my real name?"

"No. We shall tell no stories, but we shall not be communicative. You will be introduced as an old English friend of the Duchesse's."

She looked at me for an instant and there was gratitude in her expression.

When we went into the Salon I wondered what she would do. I did not speak—she took my crutch and shook up my cushion, taking great care not to touch me—I would not look up at her.

I knew that a powerful electric current would pass from my eye to hers, if I did, and that she would see that I was only longing to take her to my heart.

I remained silent and gazed into the fire. She sat down quietly on the sofa at the side, so that I would have to turn my head to look at her. Thus we remained for quite five minutes, speechless. The air throbbed with emotion—I dared not move.

At last I said, "What makes you feel all unrestful and rebellious and defiant, Alathea—am I not keeping the bargain?"

"Yes, of course."

"You are bored to death, then?"

"No—I am wondering—"

"Wondering what?"

She did not answer.

The light of the apricot lamp fell softly on her hair.

"Now tell me about what you were wondering."

Her mouth grew stubborn and she did not speak.

"It is so unlike you to do these very female things—beginning sentences and not going on. I never saw anyone so changed; once I looked upon you as the model for all that was balanced, and unlike your sex—it was I who used to feel nervous and ineffectual.

"Now, ever since we have been engaged, you seem to be disturbed, and to have lost your serenity.

"Don't you think that as it is the first evening we are alone together, it would be a wise thing to try and get at each other's point of view? Tell me the truth, Alathea, what has caused the alteration in you?"

Now she looked straight at me, and there was defiance in her expressive eyes.

"That is just what I was wondering about. It is true, I seem to have lost my serenity—I am self-conscious—I am conscious of you."

A delicious sensation of joy flowed through me—and the feeling of triumph began which is with me still. If she is conscious of me! . . .

"You were uneasy because you did not trust me, you thought underneath there might be some trap, and that I would seize you once you belonged to me.

"There was a moment when I might have felt inclined to do so, though I would never have broken my word; but you have cured me of all that, and there is nothing to prevent our being quite good acquaintances, even if your prejudice does not ever allow you to be friends."

For a second a blank look came into her expression. I was banking on my knowledge of the psychology of a human mind—the predatory instinct must inevitably be aroused in her by my attitude of indifference—if I can only act well enough to keep it up!

I should certainly win in a fairly short space of time. But she is so attractive, I do not yet know if I shall have the strength of mind to do so.

"Are you not going to give me some regular work to do each day?" she asked with a tone of mock respect in her voice. "None of the letters have been answered lately—or the bills paid."

"Yes. I scrambled through them all myself while I was waiting—but if you will look over the book again—we might finally send it to a publisher."

"Very well."

"I don't want you to feel that you have ever to stay in or do any work you don't feel inclined for. We shall have lots of time, for the rest of our lives.

"Naturally you will want to go for walks and drives, and shopping. You don't imagine that I shall expect you to be a prisoner just waiting on my beck and call!"

"Yes, that is how I took the bargain. It is quite unfair otherwise. I am here as a paid dependent, and receiving really too high wages for any possible work I can give in return.

"I would not have entered into it otherwise, or on any other terms—I loathe to receive favours."

She flashed blue sparks at me.

"I am not forced to command you to work, you know," I went on. "That is not part of the bargain. The bargain is entirely concerned with my not asking *you* to give me any favours—personal favours—like affection or caresses, etcetera, or that I shall ever expect you to be really my wife."

She frowned.

"Well, you may put your mind entirely at rest. You have been so awfully disagreeable to me for so long—ever since we were at Versailles in the summer—that you don't attract me at all now, except your intellect and your playing.

"So if you will talk sometimes, and play sometimes, that will be all right. I don't desire anything else. Now—assured about this—can't you be at ease and restful again?"

I know why she wore glasses—she cannot control the expression of her eyes! The pupils dilate and contract and tell one wonderful things! I know that this attitude of mine is having a powerful effect upon her.

The feminine in her hates to feel that she has lost power over me—even over my senses.

I could have laughed aloud I was so pleased with my success, but I did not dare to look at her much, or I could never have kept the game up. She was more delectable than I can ever describe.

"It would interest me so much to know why your hands used to be so red," I asked after a little pause. "They are getting so much whiter now."

"I had work to do—dishes to wash—our old nurse was ill too, as well as my mother—and my little brother, and then—" There was a break in her soft voice. "I do not like red hands any more than you do. I will try to take care of them now."

"Yes—do."

The evening post had come in, and been put by Burton discreetly on a side table. He naturally

thought such mundane things could not interest
me on my wedding night. I caught sight of the little pile, and asked Alathea to bring them to me.

She did, and saw that two of them were in
female writing—the rest were bills and business.

"Do you permit me to open them?" I asked
punctiliously.

"Of course," and she reddened. "Are you not
master here, how absurd to ask me!"

"It is not—you are Lady Thormonde—even if
you are not my wife—and have a right to courtesy—"

She shrugged her shoulders.

"Why did you put 'To Alathea, from her husband' on the bracelets. You are Sir Nicholas, and
not my husband."

"It was a *bêtise*—a slip of the pen, I admit,
you are right." Indifferently I opened one of the
letters, smiling over it. I put up my hand as if to
shade my eye, and looked at Alathea through the
fingers.

She was watching me with an expression of
slightly anxious interest—I could almost have believed that she was jealous!

My triumph increased.

"Perhaps we each have friends which might
bore the other—so when you want to have parties,
tell me, and I will arrange to go out, and when I
want to, I will tell you—in that way we can
never have any jars."

"Thank you—but I have no friends except the
Duchesse—or very humble people who don't
want to come to parties."

"But you will be making plenty of new
friends now. I have some which you will meet out
in the world which I dare say you won't care

about—and some who come and dine with me
sometimes, whom probably you would dislike."

"Yes—I know."

"How do you know?" I asked innocently, af-
fecting surprise.

"I used to hear them when I was typing."

I smiled—I did not defend them.

"If you should chance to meet, would you be
civil to them?"

"Of course."

Her voice was contemptuously amused and
indifferent, but her little nostrils quivered. Underneath she was disturbed, I knew.

"Do they dine often? Because I could perhaps
arrange to go and have my music lesson with
Monsieur Trani on those evenings. Twice a week,
or oftener?"

"You would refuse to meet them?" I pretended to be annoyed.

"Certainly not. One does not do ridiculous
things like that. I will meet whomever you wish.
I only thought it might spoil your pleasure if I
was there.

"Unless of course you have told them that I
am only a permanent secretary masquerading
under the name of your wife so that they need
not restrain themselves."

Her face had become inscrutable. She was
quite calm now. I grew uncertain again for a
moment. Had I carried the bluff far enough?

"They have all quite charming manners, but,
as you imply, they might not be so amused to
come to the dinner of a married man. I think the
last part of your speech was rather a reflection
upon my sense of being a gentleman though.

"I of course have not informed anyone of our

quaint relations; but I remember you told me once you did not think I was a gentleman, so I must not be offended now."

She did not speak, she was looking down and her eyelashes made a shadow on her cheeks—her mouth was sad.

Suddenly something pathetic about her touched me—she is such a gallant little fighter. She has had such an ugly cruel life—and oh!—God, is she growing to love me?

And soon shall I be able to tell her that I worship the ground she walks on, and appreciate her proud spirit and great self-respect? But I cannot chance anything—I must go on and follow what I know to be sound psychological reasoning.

I felt my will weakening then, she looked so perfectly exquisite there in the corner of the sofa. We were alone—it was nearly ten o'clock at night—the flowers were scenting the air—the lights were soft—the dinner had been perfection.

After all, I am a man—and she legally belongs to me. I felt the blood rushing wildly in my veins—I had to clench my hands and shut my eye.

"I expect you are tired now," I said a little breathlessly, "so I will say good-night, Milady, and hope that you will sleep well the first night in your new home."

I got up and she came forward quickly to hand me my crutch.

"Good-night," she whispered quite low, but she never looked at me—then she turned and went slowly from the room, never glancing back.

When she had gone, instead of going to bed I once more sank into my chair—I felt queerly faint —my nerves are not sound yet, I expect.

Well, what a strange wedding night!

Burton's face was a mask when he came to undress me. Among the many strange scenes he has witnessed and assisted at—after forty years spent in ministering to the caprices of the aristocracy—I believe he thinks this is the strangest!

* * *

The day after my marriage I did not come into the Salon until just before luncheon, at half past twelve o'clock. My bride was not there.

"Her Ladyship has gone out walking, Sir Nicholas," Burton informed me, as he settled me in my chair.

I took up a book which was lying upon the table. It was a volume of Laurence Hope's *Last Poems*.

It was not cut all through, but someone had cut it up to the eighty-sixth page and had evidently paused to read a poem called "Listen, Beloved"—the paper-knife lay between the leaves.

Whoever it was must have read it over and over, for the book opened easily there, and my eye travelled to the bottom of the page—

> Or has my spirit a divine prevision
> Of vast vague passions, stored in days to be
> When some strong souls shall conquer their
>   division
> And two shall be as one, eternally?

We are both strong souls; shall we have the strength to conquer outside things and be really "one eternally"?

Alathea must have been looking at this not an hour or more ago—what did it make her think of? I wonder.

I determined to ask her to read the whole poem presently, when we should be sitting together in the afternoon.

It had come on to rain and was a wretched dismal day. I wondered why Alathea had gone out. Probably she is as restless as I am, and being free to move, she can express her mood in rapid walking!

I began to plan my course of action—

To go on disturbing her as much as possible.

To give her the impression that I once thought her perfection, but that she herself has disillusioned me and that I am indifferent to her now.

That I have friends who divert me—and that I really only want her to be a secretary and companion—and that any interest I may show in her is merely for my own vanity, because she is, to the world, my wife!

If I can only keep this up, and not soften should I see her distressed, and not weaken or give the show away, I must inevitably win the game—perhaps sooner than I dare hope!

I felt glad that she had not been there, so that I could pull myself together, and put my armour on—so to speak—before we met.

I heard her come in just before luncheon and go to her room, and then she came on to the sitting-room without her hat.

She appeared adorable; and now that I can observe her at leisure, she seems extremely young —the childish outline, and the perfect curve of the little cheek! She does not look over eighteen years old, in spite of the firm mouth and serene manner.

I had the poems in my hand.

"I see you have been reading these," I remarked after we had given each other a cold good-morning.

The pupils of her eyes contracted for a second—she was annoyed with herself that she had left the paper-cutter in the book.

"Yes."

"After lunch will you read to me?"

"Of course."

"You like poetry?"

"Yes—some."

"This kind?"

Her cheeks became softly pink.

"Yes, I do—I dare say I should have more classical tastes, but these seem real, these poems —as if the author had meant and felt what she was writing about.

"I am no judge of poetry in the abstract, I only like it if it expresses some truth, and some thought—which appeals to me."

This was quite a long speech for her!

"Then poems about love appeal to you?" I asked, surprised.

"Why not?"

"Why not, indeed—only you always have seemed so austere and aloof, I hardly thought such a subject would have interested you!"

She gave a little shrug of her shoulders.

"Have you ever been in love?"

She laughed softly—the first time I have ever heard her laugh—it gave me a thrill.

"I don't think so! I have never talked to any men—I mean men of our class."

This relieved me.

"But you dream?"

"Not seriously."

Burton announced luncheon at that moment, and we went in.

We spoke of the rain, and she said she liked being out in the wet. She had walked all down the Avenue Henri Martin to the Bois. We spoke of the war news and the political situation—and at last we were alone again, in the Salon.

"Now read, will you, please?"

I lay back in my chair and shaded my eye with my hand.

"Do you want any special poem?"

"Read several, and then get to 'Listen, Beloved'—there is a point in it I want to discuss with you."

She took the book and settled herself with her back to the window, a little behind me.

"Come forward, please. It is more comfortable to listen when one can see the reader."

She rose reluctantly, and pulled her chair nearer to me and the fire—then she began. She chose those poems the least sensuous, and the more abstract. I watched her all the time.

I realised with a quiver of delight that she is the most passionate creature—of course she is, with that father and mother! Wait until I have awakened her enough, and she will break through all the barriers of convention and reserve, and pride. . . .

Ah! That will be a moment!

"Now read 'Listen, Beloved.' "

She turned the pages, found it, and began, and when she reached the four lines which had so interested me, she looked up for a second, and her lovely eyes were misty and far away.

Her voice is the most beautiful I have ever heard—modulated, expressive, filled with vibrant vitality and feeling—but this is the first time she has read anything appertaining to love.

Suddenly I found myself becoming suffused with emotion.

Why all the delay, the fencing, the fighting, to obtain this desired thing! This woman—my mate!

That she is my mate I know. My mate because my love is not based upon the senses alone, but is founded upon reverence and respect. I hope —I believe—I *am certain* that we shall one day realise the truth of the words—

When some strong souls shall conquer their
    division,
And two shall be as one, eternally!
Finding at last upon each other's breast
Unutterable calm and infinite rest.

For me, that means love—not the mere gratifying of the hunting instinct—not the mere primitive passion of the longed-for body—but a union of the souls, which can be satisfied, having soared beyond the laws of change.

Oh! My loved one—do not make me wait too long! ...

Ye Gods! What a state of exaltation I was in when I wrote those lines last night! But they are the truth, even if I now laugh at my expansion!

I wonder how many men are romantic underneath like I am and ashamed to show it?

When Alathea had finished the verses for the second time, she again dropped the book in her lap.

"What is your conception of love?" I asked casually.

"As I shall always have to crush it out of my life from now onward; I would rather not contemplate what my conception of it might have been."

"Why must you crush it out?" I asked blandly.

"Your fidelity to me was not part of the bargain—fidelity has to do with sex relationships, which do not concern us.

"One would not ask a secretary to become a nun, on account of one. One would only ask her to behave decently, so as not to shock the world's idea of the situation she was supposed to be filling."

Her face grew subtle.

"Then I may take a lover—someday—if I desire to?" she asked a little cynically.

"Certainly—if you tell me about it, and don't deceive me, or make me look ridiculous."

She looked straight into my eye now and hers were a little fierce.

"And you—shall you take—a mistress?"

"Possibly," I answered lazily, as though the matter were too much a foregone conclusion to discuss. "Should you mind?"

A faint movement showed in her throat, as if she had stopped herself from swallowing. She looked down—I know she finds it very difficult to lie and could not possibly do so if we were gazing at each other.

"Why should I mind?"

"No, of course, why should you?"

She looked up then, but not at me—her eyes flashed, and her lip curled in contempt.

She rose from her chair and went to the window. "If you are going to rest now—I would wish to go out." Her voice was a little hoarse.

"Yes—do go—and if you will be near the Rue

de la Paix, go into Roberts, and ask if the new menthol preparation has come, and if so, bring it back to me—it takes ages for things to be sent now."

"I was not going to the Rue de la Paix—I was going to—a hospital."

"Never mind, then—and don't hurry back, Burton will give me my tea. So *au revoir* until dinner, Milady."

I had to say all this because I was at breaking point, and could not any longer have kept up the game, but would have made an ignominious surrender, and told her I loved her—and loathed the idea of a mistress—and would certainly murder any lover she should ever even glance at!

She went from the room without a word more. And left alone I tried to sleep, but it was no good—I was too excited. I don't think I am such a fool as to flatter myself—I am trying to look at the situation abstractedly.

It seems to me that Alathea is certainly interested in me—certainly jealous and furious with herself for being so—really convinced now that she has lost her hold upon me and is uneasy, rebellious, disturbed—and unhappy!

All this is perfectly splendid—my darling little girl!

After a while I went to sleep in my chair, and was awakened by Burton coming in to turn on the lamps.

"Her Ladyship has ordered tea in her room, Sir Nicholas," he told me. "Shall I bring yours here?"

"Her Ladyship has come in, then?" I said.

"Her Ladyship did not go out, Sir," Burton answered, surprised.

What did this mean? I wondered. But I saw no sign of Alathea until she came in ready for dinner as the clock struck eight.

She was pale, but perfectly composed; she had evidently been having some battle with herself and had won.

All through dinner she talked more politely and indifferently than she has for a long time. She was brilliantly intelligent, and I had a most delightful repast. We both came up to the scratch, I think.

She longs to visit Italy, she told me; she has not been there since she was a child. I said I would take her directly war should be over, and things in the way of travel became possible again.

How strong her will must be to have so mastered herself—no slightest sign of emotion, one way or another, showed now.

She was the serene, aloof companion of the day at Versailles, before Suzette's shadow fell upon us. I grew puzzled, as the evening wore on— and just a little unsure of myself.

Had I gone too far? Had I over-disgusted her? Had all interest died out, and so is she enabled to fulfil the bargain without any more disturbance of mind?

I asked her to play to me at last, I was growing so apprehensive—and she went from one divine thing to another, for quite an hour, and then at ten o'clock stopped and said a dignified and casual "Good-night," leaving me sitting in my chair.

I heard twelve and one strike after I too went to bed—no sleep would come—I was reviewing things, and strengthening my courage. Then I got up and hobbled into the Salon to get the *Last Poems*.

The door was open—why, I don't know—nor do I know what impelled me to go out into the passage and towards Alathea's room—some powerful magnet seemed to draw me.

The carpets are very deep and soft—no noise of footfalls can be heard. I crept near the door and stopped—what was that faint sound? I listened—yes, it was a sob. I crept nearer.

Alathea was crying.

A wild sense of triumph and power and satisfaction filled me!

Is it possible that the primitive instinct of the joy of conquest could make of me such a brute?

Chapter
Ten

Marriage is the most turbulent state I could have imagined—whether or not Alathea and I will ever get the tangle straightened out I am not certain.

Now, as I write—Saturday afternoon, the ninth of November, 1918—it looks as if we have parted forever—and I am so irritated and angry that as yet I feel no grief.

The quarrel all arose from my fault, I suppose. When Alathea came into the sitting-room at about ten o'clock she had blue circles round her eyes—and knowing what caused them, I determined to ask her about them and disturb her as much as possible! This was mean of me.

"You poor child! You look as if you have been crying all night. I do hope nothing is troubling you?"

Her cheeks flushed.

"Nothing, thank you."

"Your room cannot be properly aired then, or something. I have never seen you looking so wretchedly—I wish you would be frank with me. Something must have worried you. People don't look like that for nothing."

She clasped her hands together.

"I hate this talk about—me; what does it matter how I look, or am, so long as I do the things I am engaged for?"

I shrugged my shoulders. "I suppose it ought not to, but one has a feeling that one hates anyone under one's roof to be unhappy."

"I am not unhappy—I mean, not more unhappy than I have always had to be."

"But the causes which made you sad before have been removed, surely—only things which are occurring now from day to day between you and me can bring fresh trouble—is it something I have done?"

Silence.

"Alathea, if you knew how you exasperate me by your silence! I was always taught that it was very rude not to answer when one was spoken to."

"It depends upon who speaks, and what about, and whether they have a right to an answer."

"Then the implication is that I have no right to an answer, when you are silent?"

"Probably."

I grew irritated.

"Well, I think that I have a right. I ask you a plain question—Have I done anything which has caused you distress—distress which is so evident that you must have been crying?"

She threw up her arms.

"Why on earth cannot you keep to business? It is quite unfair—if I were really your secretary, and nothing more, you would never persecute me for answers like this!"

"Yes, I would. I have a perfect right to know why anyone in my service is unhappy. Your fencing tells me that it *is* something which I have done which has hurt you, and I insist upon knowing what it is."

"I shall not tell you," defiantly.

"I am very angry with you, Alathea." My voice was stern.

"I don't care!" Hers was passionate.

"I think you are very rude."

"You have told me that before—well, I am rude, then! I will tell you nothing. I will do nothing but just be your servant and obey orders which relate to the work I have been engaged for."

I felt so furious I had to lie back in my chair and shut my eye.

"You have a very poor sense of a bargain—if you only keep it in the letter. Your constant underneath hostility makes everything so difficult.

"The implication of your whole attitude towards me—and of everything you say and do— is that you feel injured, that you have some grudge against me."

I tried to speak levelly.

"What on earth have I ever done to you except treat you with every courtesy?—except that one day when you had the baby in your arms and I was rude, but apologised.

"And that one other time when I kissed you —and God knows I was sorry enough afterwards and have regretted it ever since. What *is* the reason of your attitude? It is absolutely unfair."

This seemed to upset her considerably. She hated the idea that she was thought unfair. It may have made her realise too that she *had* a definite sense of injury. She lost her temper—she stamped her scrap of a foot.

"I hate you!" she burst out. "You and your bargain! I wish I were dead!" And then she sank into the sofa and covered her face with her hands, and by the shaking of her shoulders I saw that she was crying!

If I had been cool enough to think then, I suppose I could have reasoned that all this was probably most flattering to me, and an extra proof of her state of mind; but the agitation it had plunged me into made me unable to balance things.

I too allowed my temper to get the better of me, and I got up as best I could, and, seizing my crutch, I walked towards my bedroom door.

"I shall expect an apology," was all I said, and went in and left her alone.

If we are to go on fighting like this, life won't be worth living!

I tried to calm myself, and went to the window; but the servants came into the room to make the bed—so I was forced to go back again to the sitting-room. Alathea had gone into the little Salon, I suppose, because, for the same reason, she could not have returned to her room.

I sat down in my chair quite exhausted. I did not feel like reading or doing anything.

It was today that we were to go to the Duchesse's in the afternoon for Alathea to be presented to our friends as my wife! I wondered if she had forgotten this!

After an hour Burton came in with the second post.

"You do look badly, Sir Nicholas!" he said. His face was perplexed and troubled. "Can I get you anything?"

"Where is Her Ladyship, Burton?"

Then he told me that she had gone out—I could see he wanted to say something—his remarks are generally valuable.

"Out with it, Burton."

"I do think it is Mamzelle that's causing all the trouble—as bad luck would have it, as I opened the door to let Her Ladyship out, who should come up the stair a moment after but Mamzelle!

"They must have passed on the floor below. Neither had took the lift, which, as you know, Sir Nicholas, is out of order again, since last night."

"Then she thinks Suzette has come in here to see me, Burton. By Jove, what a devilish complication! I think we had better move from the flat as quickly as we can—"

"It seems as if it would be advisable, Sir Nicholas."

"Can you suggest anything, Burton? I really am quite knocked over today."

"Her Ladyship don't chat to servants like some ladies—or I could easily let her maid know that Mamzelle don't visit here—so that won't do," he mused. "You could not tell her yourself straight out, Sir Nicholas, could you?"

"It would be difficult—because it presupposes I think she minds about it, and for me to let her know that would insult her more than anything."

"Beg pardon, Sir Nicholas, but there was a young woman some twenty years ago—who had a temper, like—and I always found it was best just to make a fuss of her, and not do no reasoning—that is what they wants, Sir Nicholas—indeed it is.

"I've watched them in all classes for a matter of many years—you can get what you want of them if you only make a fuss of them."

"What does 'to make a fuss of' exactly mean, Burton?"

"Well, it is not for me to tell you, Sir—knowing ladies as you do—but it is just kissing and fondling them, and them things, makin' them feel that they're just everything—even reasonable, Sir Nicholas."

Burton's dryly humorous face delighted me. His advice was first-class, too!

"I'll think over it," I told him, and he left me alone.

That would be one way of winning or losing everything certainly!—but it would also be breaking my word, and I don't believe I could do that.

Alathea came in in time for luncheon. Her face was set in a mutinous, obstinate mould. We went into the dining-room immediately, and so there was no chance of conversation. I noticed that she wore no bracelets or rings—nothing of mine, not even the wedding ring.

We were icy to each other during the meal, and made small conversation, and when we were alone with the coffee I just said—

"I hope that you have not forgotten that at four o'clock we are to go to the Duchesse's to meet the friends that she thinks it is suitable for you to know."

Alathea started. I could see she had not registered this fact for this date.

"I would rather not go," she said resentfully.

"I dare say you would—so would I—but we owe the Duchesse gratitude for all her kindness to us, and I fear we must."

We did not speak further—I could not talk until she apologised—and I rose to go out of the room. She gave me my crutch. Her not apologising made me burn with resentment.

I had not been in the Salon a minute, however, before she came in, her face crimson. She
stood in front of me.

"I apologise for showing temper this morning.
Would it not do after today if I just lived out
somewhere, and came in and worked as before?
It is a perfect farce that I live here, and wear a
wedding ring—even the servants must be laughing at me."

"I notice you do not wear a wedding ring.
Your whole attitude is perfectly impossible, and
I demand an explanation. What is the reason of
it? . . . We made a bargain—and you are not keeping it."

"If you will give me time to work, I will pay
you back the fifty thousand francs—and the
clothes and jewels I can leave behind me—I
want to go. . . ."

She spoke with a break in her voice now.

"Why do you want to go suddenly?—there is
nothing different today from yesterday or any other day. I refuse to be the puppet of your caprices."

She stood clasping and unclasping her hands,
never looking at me.

"Alathea," I said sternly, "look me straight
in the face and tell me the truth. *What* is your
reason?"

"I can't." Still her eyes were down.

"Is there someone else?" My voice sounded
fierce to my own ears. I had a sudden fear.

"But you said it would not matter if there was
someone else—if I told you," she answered defiantly.

"There is someone else, then?" I tried to be
casual. "Look at me."

Slowly she raised her eyes until they met my one.

"No—there is no one. I just don't want to live here—in this flat—any longer."

"Unless you can give me some definite reason for this extraordinary behaviour on your part, I am afraid I must refuse to discuss the situation, and meanwhile will you please go to your room and fetch the rings and bracelets."

She turned and left without a word—I dare say she wondered what I was going to do with them.

She brought them back.

"Come here close."

She came rebelliously.

"Give me your hand."

"I won't."

"Alathea—I will seize it—cripple as I am—and make you obey me by force if you will not for asking."

Her whole face expressed furious resentment, but she is too sensible and level-headed to make a scene, so she gave me her hand. I put the wedding ring back—and the big diamond one.

"Now you will wear them until you convince me of your reason so thoroughly that I myself take them off—the bracelets you can do as you like about, throw them away, or give them to your maid.

"And this afternoon I hope I can count upon your instincts of being a lady to make you behave so that no one can chatter about us."

She drew away her hand, as though my touch burnt her; her expression was contemptuously haughty.

"Of course you can count upon me—for this

afternoon," and she turned and went out of the
room again.

And now I am waiting for her to come back
dressed for the Duchesse's reception—it is ten
minutes to four o'clock—the volcano upon which
we are living cannot go on simmering much longer, there is bound to be an explosion soon!

* * *

Later. Things are developing! My bride and
I never spoke a word on the way to the Hotel de
Courville. She was looking the most desirable mor-
sel a man would wish to present to his friends.

The sable cloak and the most perfect frock
and hat. Her maid is evidently a splendid hair-
dresser. She was "of a *chic*," as Maurice afterwards told me.

I had telephoned and broken the news to him
while I was waiting for Alathea to come. He was
not surprised, he pretended to be delighted about
it.

The Duchesse kissed us both fondly, and said
many pleasant things, and having placed me in a
suitable chair, brought everyone to me, and presented Alathea to them all.

They none of them could find fault with the
appearance of my wife, nor her manner. She had
the ways of the Ancien Régime, like the Duchesse. I could see that she was having a huge success.

While everything seemed to be going beautifully, my dear old friend came to me.

"It is not progressing, Nicholas—*hein?*"

"There is something very wrong, Duchesse."

"*Tiens!* . . . She is jealous of someone, Nicholas—it is not possible that you have still—?"

"No, indeed—that is over long ago—but I do believe she thinks it is not."

"And you cannot tell her—?"

"I am not supposed to know it would matter to her!"

"*Bon* . . . Do you really love the child, Nicholas?"

"*Chère amie*—with my whole heart—I only want her in all the world."

"And she is being impossible for you surely! I know her character—if she thinks you have a mistress—her pride is of *le diable!*"

"It is indeed. . . ."

The Duchesse laughed.

"We must see what can be done—dear boy."

At that moment the crowd returned from the other room and the Duchesse rose and left me.

At last the whole thing was over, and Maurice and I had a cigarette together in the tea-room.

"People would be crazy—'simply crazy—my dear chap'—about Alathea," he told me. She was *seduisante*—how right I had been! How fortunate I was! When was I going to England?

He said farewells after this, and once more *my wife* and I were alone in the brougham.

Alathea wore her mask. Having been received now as my wife and by the Duchesse, whom she loves and respects, she knows she cannot go on suggesting she will not live in the flat with me.

She cannot bring herself to speak about Suzette, because the implication would be that she objects . . . I wondered if the Duchesse had been able to say anything to her.

She did not speak at all and went straight to her room when we arrived.

It was five minutes past eight when she came into the sitting-room.

"I am sorry if I have kept you waiting," were her first words.

At dinner we spoke ceremoniously of the party. And when we went back to the Salon she went straight to the piano and played divinely for an hour.

The music soothed me—I felt less angry and disturbed.

"Won't you come and speak now?" I called in a pause—and she came over and sat down.

"Don't let us talk tonight," she said. "I am trying to adjust things in my mind. I want to go to my mother tomorrow, if you will agree. She is ill again, and has not been able to start."

"I cannot understand why it should be so difficult," I replied. "The idea did not affright you when we first talked of it. You voluntarily accepted the proposal—made your bargain, promised to stick to it—and here after three days you are trying to break out.

"You are insinuating that the circumstances are too horrible for you to continue bearing it. Surely your reason and common sense must tell you that your behaviour is grotesque."

The same agitation which always shows when we talk thus overcame her again. She did not speak.

"I could understand it better if you were a hysterical character—you did not seem to be so—but now no ridiculous school miss of romance could be more given to the vapours."

This stung her to the quick, as I had meant that it should. She bounded up.

"Well—I will, then. I hate you having a mistress!"

She was trembling all over, and as white as marble.

I leaned back and laughed softly. My joy was so immense I could not help it.

"To begin with, I have no mistress, but if I had, how can it possibly matter to you, since you hate me, and yourself arrange to be only my secretary."

"You have no mistress!" I could see she thought I was lying ignobly.

"I had one, as of course you knew, but the moment I began to think that you might be an agreeable companion, I parted from her at the time when you saw the counterfoils in the cheque-book."

"Then—?" She still looked incredulous.

"She has a cousin living in the flat above, married to an *antiquaire*. She comes to see her. You have no doubt met on the stairs.

"And on our wedding day she came in here —not knowing—to thank me for a villa I had given her as a good-bye present. I am very angry that she intruded, and it shall never happen again."

"Is this true?" She was breathless.

That made me angry.

"I am not in the habit of lying," I said haughtily. "You are not unutterably shocked that I should have had—a friend—are you?"

Her face grew contemptuous.

"No—my father had one—men are all beasts."

"They may be in the abstract, but are not when they can find a woman worth love and respect."

She shrugged her shoulders.

"My mother is an angel."

"Now that your mind is at rest as to this question, have you any other cause of complaint against me? Though why it should matter to you what I do or don't do in this respect as long as I am courteous to you and fulfil my side of the bargain I cannot think. One could imagine you were jealous!"

"Jealous!" she flared furiously. "Jealous, I! How ridiculous! One has to care to be jealous!" And then she flounced out of the room.

Yes—even when they appear all that is balanced—there is nothing so amazing as a woman!

* * *

Sunday. I slept last night soundly for some strange reason, and woke quite late this morning.

I rang for Burton—it was nine o'clock.

"Has Her Ladyship breakfasted yet, Burton?"

"Her Ladyship breakfasted at eight, and left the house at half-past, Sir Nicholas."

My heart sank. I did not hurry to get up. The doctors were coming with the wonderful artist who is making my new foot, at twelve o'clock, and I am to have it on today for the first time.

This would be a surprise for Alathea when she returned to lunch. I read my journal in bed, and thought over the whole of our acquaintance. Yes, certain she has greatly changed in the last six weeks. And possibly I am nearer my goal than I could have dared to hope.

Now my method must be to be sweet to her —and not to tease her any more.

How wonderful it will be when—she does love me. I have not thought much about my own feelings lately. She has kept me so often irritated and angry—but I know that there is a steady advance and that I love her more than ever.

To see her little mutinous rebellious face softening—it will be worth all the waiting. . . . But meanwhile she is out, and I had better get up!

* * *

I wonder if all the hundreds of other fellows who lost a leg below the knee and were cripples for eighteen months felt the same as I did when the new limb was fixed, and they stood upon two feet again for the first time!

A strange, almost mad sense of exaltation filled me ... I could walk! ... I was no longer a prisoner, dependent upon the devotion of attendants.

It hurt and was awkward for a while .... But oh! the joy, joy, joy!

After the doctors and the specialist had gone with hearty congratulations, my dear old faithful servant had tears in his eyes as he dressed me.

"You must excuse me, Sir Nicholas—but I am so glad."

Excuse him! I could have hugged him in my own joy.

I wanted to run about! I wanted to shout and sing.

I wonder what Alathea will say when she sees me! I wonder if it will make any difference to her.

Tomorrow morning—they are going to put in my eye!

I became excited—there was about a quarter of an hour to wait. I tried to sit down and settle to a book—but it was useless, the words conveyed no sense—I could not even read the papers!

I began listening to every sound—there are not many things passing at this time on a Sunday morning—but of course she was walking, not driving. ... One o'clock struck—she had not returned. Burton came in to ask if I would postpone lunch.

"Her Ladyship did not say when she would be back," he said.

"We had better not wait, then—I believe now she told me she would not be in."

Burton had opened a pint of champagne. On this tremendous occasion he felt I should drink my own health.

I had begun to lose some of my joy—I wished she had been here to share it with me.

* * *

I have walked up and down—up and down. . . . It is four o'clock now, and she has not returned.

Midnight. I have spent a beastly day. My exhilaration has all evaporated now—I have had no one to share it with me. Maurice and everyone is leaving me discreetly alone, knowing I am supposed to be on my honeymoon! Honeymoon! . . .

I spent the afternoon waiting, waiting. And after tea, when Alathea had not arrived, I began taking longer turns, walking up and down the broad corridor; and at last I paused outside her room, and a desire came over me to look in on it, and see how she had arranged it.

There was silence. I listened a moment, then I opened the door.

The fire was not lit—it all seemed cold and cheerless. I turned on the light.

Except for the tortoise-shell and gold brushes and boxes I had had put on the dressing-table for her, there was not an indication that anyone stayed there—none of the usual things women have about in their rooms.

One could see that she looked upon it just as an hotel, and not a permanent abode. There were no photographs of her family—no books of her own—nothing.

Only the bracelets were on the table, still in their case, and on looking nearer I saw that there was a bottle of scent.

It had no label, and when I opened it I smelled the exquisite perfume of fresh roses that she uses—where does she get it?—it is the purest I have ever smelled in my life.

I had an insane desire to open the drawers in the chest and touch her stockings and gloves —I had a wild feeling altogether—I wanted my love—rebellious, unrelenting, anyhow! I just longed for her.

I resisted my stupidities and made myself leave the room—and then tried to feel joy again in my leg.

Burton was turning on the lamps when I got back to the Salon.

"There are rumours that something is going to happen, Sir Nicholas—talk of an Armistice I heard when I was out."

But I know all these rumours and talks, we have heard them before, so this did not affect me. I could feel nothing, as time went on, but a passionate ache. Why, why must she be so cruel to me? Why does she leave me alone?

Alathea, I would never be so unkind to you. And yet I don't know—if I were jealous and angry, as I suppose she is, I could of course be much crueller.

In despair at ten o'clock I telephoned the Hotel de Courville—

Lady Thormonde had been there in the morning, I was told, but the Duchesse had left for Hautevine at two o'clock. No one was in the house now. No—they did not know Lady Hilda Bulteel's telephone number.

Had I made some mistake? I tried to remember. She had said she meant to decide if she could bear the situation or no and that she was going to her mother—she wanted to be with her—she had been ill and could not start.

Yes, of course that is it. The mother is ill, and they have no telephone. I must wait until the morning. She cannot really mean not to come back—in any case she would then let me know.

But what an agony of suspense!

Burton came and gave me my medicine—when I was in bed—and although I knew it was a camouflaged sleeping-draught, I drank it—I just could not bear it any longer.

But I only slept until four—and now I am sitting up writing this, and I feel as if every queer force is abroad, and that all sorts of momentous things are happening. Oh, when will daylight come!

* * *

I was awakened by cannon!

I leaped from my bed—yes, leaped.

Wild with excitement, I was now wide awake!

Yes—there were cannon booming!

What was happening? . . .

Then I heard murmurs in the street. I rang the bell violently—I had slept very late—and Burton rushed in.

"An Armistice, Sir Nicholas," he cried joyously. "It's true, after all!"

An Armistice! Oh, God!

So at last, at last, we have won—and it has not been all in vain!

I shook with emotion.

I was too excited all through breakfast to feel renewed anxiety about Alathea. I was accepting the fact that she had stayed with her mother. Surely, surely she would be in soon now!

The oculist, and his artist craftsman, would be arriving soon, at eleven o'clock—if the excitement of an Armistice does not prevent them! I hope all that won't be going on when Alathea does come in!

Eleven came and with it the oculist and by luncheon time I had a second blue eye! But oh! the shouting in the streets and the passionate joy in the air!

Everything was now swallowed up in an overwhelming suspense.

What could have kept Alathea?

I walked to the glass soberly when the doctors had gone, eager to get away and join the rejoicers, and what I saw startled me.

How astonishing the art of these things is now! Unless I turn my glance in some impossible way, I have apparently two bright blue eyes with the same lids and lashes. The scrap of shrapnel only injured the orb itself, and did not touch the lid, fortunately.

And the socket had healed up miraculously in the last month. I am not now a disgusting object. Perhaps—possibly. Yes—can I induce her to love me soon?

But what is the good of it all? She has not returned and now something must be done.

But on this day of days no one could be found to attend to anything! Shops were shut, post-offices did not work. The city was mad with rejoicing.

The agony grew and grew. What if she means to leave me and has just disappeared? Not telling me on purpose to punish me?

At this thought I went frantically into her room again, and looked on the dressing-table. The ring cases were there in a drawer in the William and Mary looking-glass, but no rings.

No—if she had meant not to return, she would have left them behind her. This gave me hope.

I had the fire lit—Burton lit it—everyone else was out.

Of course the crowd has prevented her returning; there would be great difficulty in getting back from Auteuil.

At last, when I had been pacing like a restless tiger, and twilight was coming, I sank into my chair, overcome with the strain.

I did not mean to feel the drivel of self-pity, but it is a ghastly thing to be all alone and anxious, when everyone else is shouting for joy.

I was staring into the fire. I had not had the lights lit on purpose. I wanted the soft shadows to soothe me. Burton had gone down again to the concierge.

A bitterness and melancholy I cannot describe were holding me. Of what good my leg and my eye, if I am to suffer torment once more.

A sense of forsakenness held me, perhaps I dozed, because I was worn out when suddenly I was conscious of a closing door and opening my eye I saw that Alathea stood before me!

A log fell and blazed brightly and I could see that her face was greatly moved.

"I—am so sorry if you have been anxious—Burton says you have . . . I would have been back earlier, but I was caught in the crowd."

I reached out and turned on the lamp near me, and when she saw my eye and leg she fell upon her knees at my side.

"Oh! Nicholas," she cried brokenly, and I put out my hand and took hers.

* * *

Oh, what a thing is joy!

My heart beat madly, the blood rushed in my veins. What was that noise I heard in my ear beyond the shouting in the street?

Was it the cooing which used to haunt my dreams? Yes, it was. And Alathea's voice was murmuring in French—

"Pardon, pardon, I have been so ungrateful. *Pardonnez-moi*. Forgive me! Oh, Nicholas, forgive me!"

I wanted to whisper—

"Darling, you have returned, nothing matters any more"; but I controlled myself, she must finally surrender first!

Then she sprang to her feet and stood back to look at me. I rose too and there towered above her.

"Oh, I am so glad ... so glad," she said tremulously. "How wonderful, how miraculous! It is for this great day!"

"I thought that you had left me altogether." I was a little breathless. "I was so very sad."

Now she looked down.

"Nicholas"—how I loved to hear her pronounce my name!—"Nicholas, I have heard from my mother of your great generosity. You had helped us without ever telling me, and then paid again to stop my mother's anxiety, and again to stop mine.

"Oh! I am ashamed, humbled, that I have

been as I have been to you. Forgive me, forgive me. I ask you to from my heart."

"I have nothing to forgive, child. Come, let us sit down and talk everything over." I sank into the sofa, and she came beside me.

She would not look at me, however, but her little face was gentle and shy.

"I cannot understand, though, why you did all that. I cannot understand anything about it all ... you do not love me. You only wanted me for your secretary, and yet you paid over a hundred thousand francs! The generosity is great."

I gazed and gazed at her.

"And you hate me," I said as coolly as I could, "and let me buy you, so that you could save your family—your sacrifice was immense."

Suddenly she looked straight up at me—her eyes so filled with passion that wild fire kindled in my blood.

"Nicholas, I do not hate you."

I took both her hands and drew her to me, while outside in the street they were singing the "Marseillaise" and yelling for joy.

"Alathea, tell me the truth—what, then, do you feel?"

"I don't know, I wanted to murder Suzette. Perhaps you can tell me, here in your arms!"

And with wild abandon she fell forward into my fond embrace.

Ah! God! The bliss of the next few moments! With her soft lips pressed to mine—then I could not repeat often enough that I loved her, nor make her tell me how she loved me in return!

Afterwards, I grew masterful—and ordered her to recount to me everything from the very beginning.

Yes—she had been attracted by me from the

first day—but she hated the friends I had round me, and she did not like the aimlessness of my life.

"Whenever I used to be growing too contemptuous, though, Nicholas, I used to remember the V.C., and then the feeling went off, but I was growing angrier and angrier with myself because in spite of believing you only thought of me as one of them, I could not prevent myself from loving you.

"There is something about you that made me forget all about your leg and your eye!"

"Those cheques disgusted you!" and I kissed the little curl by her ear. She was clasped close to me now. "That was the beginning of my determination to conquer you and have you for my own!"

She caressed my hair.

"I adore thick hair, Nicholas," she whispered —"but now you have had enough flattery! I am off to dress!"

She struggled and pretended she wanted to leave me, but I would not let her go.

"Only when *I* please, and at a price! I want to show you that you have a husband who, in spite of a wooden leg and a glass eye, is a powerful brute!"

"I love you strong like that!" she cooed—her eyes soft with passion again. "I am not good really, or austere or cold!"

And I knew it was true as she paid the toll with a kiss.

Presently I made her let me come and choose which frock she was to put on for dinner, and I insisted that I should stay and see her hair being brushed, and the maid, Henriette, with her French eye, beamed upon us understandingly!

While Burton almost cried with happiness when I told him Her Ladyship and I were friends again.

"I knew it, Sir Nicholas, if you'd just make a fuss of her."

How right he was!

What a dinner we had, gay as two children, fond and foolish as sweethearts always are—and then the afterwards!

"Let us go and see the streets," my little love implored. "I feel that we should shout our divine happiness with the crowd!"

But when we went out on the balcony to investigate, we saw that it would be impossible— I am not yet steady enough on my feet to have faced that throng.

So we stood there and sang and cheered with them as they swept on towards the Arc de Triomphe, and gradually a delirious intoxication held us both, and I drew her back into the softly lighted room.

"Lover!" she whispered as she melted into my arms, and all I answered was, "Soul of Mine."

And now I know what the verse means:

And two shall be as one, eternally.

ABOUT THE AUTHOR

BARBARA CARTLAND, the celebrated romantic author, historian, playwright, lecturer, political speaker and television personality, has now written over 150 books. Miss Cartland has had a number of historical books published and several biographical ones, including that of her brother, Major Ronald Cartland, who was the first Member of Parliament to be killed in the War. This book had a Foreword by Sir Winston Churchill.

In private life, Barbara Cartland, who is a Dame of the Order of St. John of Jerusalem, has fought for better conditions and salaries for Midwives and Nurses. As President of the Royal College of Midwives (Hertfordshire Branch), she has been invested with the first Badge of Office ever given in Great Britain, which was subscribed to by the Midwives themselves. She has also championed the cause for old people and founded the first Romany Gypsy Camp in the world.

Barbara Cartland is deeply interested in Vitamin Therapy and is President of the British National Association for Health.

Barbara Cartland

The world's bestselling author of romantic fiction.
Her stories are always captivating tales of intrigue,
adventure and love.

☐	A VERY NAUGHTY ANGEL	2107	$1.25
☐	CALL OF THE HEART	2140	$1.25
☐	AS EAGLES FLY	2147	$1.25
☐	THE TEARS OF LOVE	2148	$1.25
☐	THE DEVIL IN LOVE	2149	$1.25
☐	THE ELUSIVE EARL	2436	$1.25
☐	A DREAM FROM THE NIGHT	2972	$1.25
☐	THE BORED BRIDEGROOM	6381	$1.25
☐	THE PENNILESS PEER	6387	$1.25
☐	THE LITTLE ADVENTURE	6428	$1.25
☐	LESSONS IN LOVE	6431	$1.25
☐	THE DARING DECEPTION	6435	$1.25
☐	CASTLE OF FEAR	8103	$1.25
☐	THE RUTHLESS RAKE	8240	$1.25
☐	THE DANGEROUS DANDY	8280	$1.25
☐	THE WICKED MARQUIS	8467	$1.25
☐	LOVE IS INNOCENT	8505	$1.25
☐	THE FRIGHTENED BRIDE	8780	$1.25
☐	THE FLAME IS LOVE	8887	$1.25

Barbara Cartland

The world's bestselling author of romantic fiction. Her stories are always captivating tales of intrigue, adventure and love.